A Time for Lepralites

A Time for Lepralites

by AngJon Hornibrook

A catalogue record for this book is available from the British Library.

eBook ISBN: 978-1-3999-7329-8

Paperback ISBN: 978-1-3999-6468-5

Authored, Illustrated, Edited, and Typeset by AngJon Hornibrook, a collaboration between Deirdre Tobin and Angele & Jonathan Hornibrook

Cover Design by Liam Fitzgerald www.frequency.studio

For more information, visit www.lepralites.com

and

Author's Facebook page

Dedicated to all cancer survivors worldwide.

Table of Contents

Acknowledgments

A huge thank you to my wife, Angele. You spent many long hours trying to interpret some of the strange creatures that were popping out of my imagination and translating them into your hand-drawn pictures for the story's web page and the illustrations you see in this book. I thank the Lord every day for you being in my life.

A special thank you to you D.

To Deirdre Tobin, thank you for your friendship with my wife and me during the health battles our family endured over the last year and for your relentless ongoing mission of dragging my writing mechanisms from scribe to 2023 technology. Believe me when I say I did not go down without a fight. Time is a precious thing, and I thank you for sharing so much of yours with us.

To The Cork University Hospital oncology unit, with Professor P. Redmond and all its outstanding staff, and to The South infirmary Oncology department, with Professor Seamus O Reilley and the fantastic, beautiful staff, who treated Angele. Thank you so much for saving her life.

To Liam of Frequency Studios, Crosshaven, Cork. Thank you for all your advice in the whole writing process and especially for your unique designs of a great book cover and fantastic website. You have brought my vision of the book and its theme to life. You truly have excellent skills.

To my ever-present and always loving Mum, Rosemary Hornibrook/ Beamish. Thank you for being who you are. And thank you for being part of our lives.

Prologue. Land of Adam's Forefathers

The washing machine ground a high-speed spin, leaving Adam frustrated, wanting to pick it up and fling it out the back door.

It could be the day of the year that haunted him.

Or else it was that he was allergic to hearing that machine drone on, as it was one of his kitchen pet hates. That and the ongoing cycle of the rolling drying drum full of clothes

reminded him that it was another soft, wet day in North Cork,

Ireland. Nevertheless, he had to finish a report and email it to head office before starting business tomorrow. His whole task seemed doomed for failure because of the constant attacks on his concentration levels by household appliances.

"It's no wonder Jane turns them on, then runs off to bed," he thought as his tired eyes were drawn again towards the turning tumble-dryer.

"Is it the way that everything in this world goes around? Is that why God made the world round? That is why no matter how far we travel, we always seem to land back where we should?"

That certainly is an ancient question that humans ask themselves.

Today, Adam was reminded by a shop customer that he was back in the land of McCarthy's clans of old. Until that moment, he had no idea something special tied his name to the Kanturk area. Was it just another one of those meant-to-be moments? Such as, why did he go out walking on a freezing morning, something he would never have done in the city, and then find the most adorable, unusual animals that would drastically change the family?

It certainly was a strange time of acceptance of new experiences for him.

"Thank goodness at least that blasted washing machine has finally stopped," he thought as he tried to refocus back on his laptop.

"Hi Adam, what are you doing?"

It was Titch-Ella.

"You are looking very down on yourself. What is wrong? Anything I can do to help?"

Once again, Adam was dismayed by the little one's behaviour, for she was showing that she was far more than any animal or child he knew. Even though Mum treated them as such, he felt himself drawn into her big ocean-blue caring eyes. He wanted to be flippant and pass her off with words such as "Yes, I'm fine, and how are you?" but the way she looked searchingly at him, he would not show her such injustice, for she was visibly waiting for him to respond. He studied her delightful strangeness, wanting to talk about something buried deep within him. Still, she paused, all of four inches tall, standing on the kitchen table with her wings relaxed. Seeing his hesitation, she asked,

"Do you mind if I sit and listen?"

It was weird for Adam having his thoughts read. Well, that is what it felt like to him at that moment.

He closed the laptop, removing his distractions from sight.

"It is now fifteen years today, and I still do not know how to deal with it. I never do. Today, fifteen years ago, my first wife passed away to your Neverland."

Titch-Ella did not speak as he took his long pause, then he said,

"Do you know that is where I met Jane?" Then he paused

again, looking for the start of a sentence,

"I will tell you how I met Mum, for if it were not for her, I would have drowned in my pit of despair. I know I should not be saying things like that to you, being so young."

Titch-Ella stopped him and said,

"Maybe? But I know well what depression is and how it damages humans. You are forgetting about our daisy chain of knowledge."

Remembering the many conversations between Hoaby, Titch-Ella, Mum, and yes also himself of the clans sharing, Adam nodded and started to speak cautiously, as if expecting someone to come through the door.

"What I am about to say to you, I hope, will not end up on the daisy chain."

Again, she did not speak as she waited for his words.

"Well, Mum had come to Ireland in the hope of getting a nursing post and was filling in her time as a care assistant in the hospital that my first wife was admitted to as she neared her time to leave us. They called it palliative care, meaning they managed Hillary's pain. That was her name. Hillary."

"We were engaged for three years, waiting for the right time to get married. What a waste of three years, and it was all my decision. Not enough money, no house, and so on. I had all the right excuses but at the wrong time. Eventually, we had set a date for six months, after Hillary had explained her thinking to me, telling me that we did not need money nor our own house to get married and how she was more than happy to marry a simple shop hand on low wages."

Adam stared into the abyss of the still churning clothes dryer as though it was a blackhole to his past, wanting to move it forward in time. Then he continued some more.

"We were just two months into our marriage, and there I stood in the hallway, waiting for her to return from the doctor.

I was waiting with flowers in hand, getting ready for the big joyful announcement waiting for her to tell me that she was pregnant with our first child as she had felt all those unusual sickly pains in her tummy. I knew something was very wrong the second she came through that door. There and then, all our dreams wilted quicker than the lilies I held in my arms.'

Adam's eyes transfixed on the rumbling machine, but his mind was fifteen years away as he carried on.

"Hillary had cancer all through her."

The silence had found a place between the tick and the tock of his passing time where nothing moved, for again, he went silent. Titch-Ella knew she had no words for him, for what could anyone say when another was reliving a moment in their past. Still, she waited as he mustered enough focus to see the little one before him.

"It did not take long for Hillary to reach her last days. We heard all the what ifs. If only you had gone to the doctor earlier. It felt like I was being blamed for not looking around corners. Why would we? Very few would be searching for signs of illness in their early thirties. I still hear Hillary's last words as she gripped my hand tighter than ever; I do not know where she got that strength from when she said Adds, that is what she used to call me, Adds now you need to go and live life for the both of us".

"Then she slipped away from me."

He began to cry and rubbed his shirt sleeve across his eyes,

"How can I live for the two of us?"

He looked to Titch-Ella for answers. She stood up and walked across the table towards him. Then, standing right in front of him, glaring into his wet eyes, said,

"But you are every day, Adam!! You are everyone's perfect husband and Daddy; you wrap your family around you like a snuggle blanket, and we all know you will never let go. That is what Hillary asked you to do."

"But she is not here," he replied, sniffling his relief back up his nose.

"Oh, Adam, surely you know that when we go to Never Never land, we are always around. We are everywhere."

Wanting him to move away from his pain, she said,

"Can you tell me about how you met Mum?"

Then she lowered her voice to a whisper,

"It's ok. Everybody is asleep, and I won't tell Mum you told me so you can tell me all the secret bits, too." Then she gave her cheeky, chubby, fur-filled smile and sat down again before him.

"Where will I start?" he asked himself aloud.

" Mum was the sweet carer who held Hillary's hand when I was not there. She was the light in that somber room for the two weeks as life disappeared. At first, I never noticed her, for I was trying to accept that my world was being taken from me. but one morning, Hillary said that she would love to have the inner strength that the nurse who was looking after her had. I never asked why she would make such a statement; was it the fact that she was feeling so worn down herself? But it did draw my attention to see a person with a vast depth of love in her, and over the remaining days, she became a friend to us both. Friendship was the most incredible gift Mum ever gave me."

"When Hillary did pass, I never asked her to come to the funeral, but as I stood in that lonely churchyard after laying my life in the ground, I saw her walk out the church gate. She gave me a brief smile of assurance, and then she was gone."

Titch-Ella was crying now, too, as her heart was breaking for Adam. He had lost his wife, and now their friend Jane was disappearing too from his life. The more she understood what it must have felt like for him, the more her tears fell.

Adam continued to explain past travelled roads.

"Life for me had changed forever. There I was at only thirty-six years of age and a widower. I spent the following months doing what I did best, hiding from life while going through the motions of work and going back to our old flat to cry over various bits of memories that Hillary had left around the place."

"One day, a woman entered the shop where I was working. She was selling Daffodils, raising money for cancer research. On hearing my story, she spoke of various fundraising methods for the cause. Well, I can tell you, it was like being hit by a bolt of lightning. Yes, I had lost Hillary, but what about all those people who are still alive and fighting the illness? I decided there and then that I, too, would join the battle. So, I got my sponsorship forms and started training for the upcoming city marathon. Now, you need to understand when I got that card to fill; two things were going through my head. One, how am I supposed to fill it with sponsors' names and raise my two-thousand-euro limit that I set for myself to raise, and secondly, how am I supposed to get myself fit enough, that I won't end up making a clown of myself in front of the crowds that always gathered for this event."

"To cut a long story short, with lots of walking and trotting and then more trotting than walking, I managed to get my body fooled enough that it would think that it would be ready for the long run. Would you believe there were over three thousand in sponsorships on my card waiting to be collected once I managed to get over that finish line, most, given by people who would have known Hillary?"

"The big day arrived. Many thousands of people were all ready to run the twenty-six miles. I was all dressed in my yellows. As I looked around on the starting line, I could see many others with their purple and blue charity colours. The starter hooter sounded, and I trotted off down the road, feeling good about myself for doing so well. The miles began to pass, and I was surprised at how fit I felt. I was setting my slow, realistic pace for a novice and doing fine until about mile number eighteen. That is when that wall, everybody had told me, would start to bite."

"Walls don't bite, do they?"

Adam paused, almost surprised by her voice, as though he had forgotten that Titch-Ella was there. He fumbled with his words for a moment, then continued with his explanation for her,

"It is when the body starts to tell us we can't go any further."

"That happened to me too," she responded, "when we were on our way to find Doadi, that was not a nice feeling. My tummy felt so fat I could not go any further."

Then she smiled at Adam, willing him to continue. He nodded, smiling at the simplicity of her understanding, and continued.

"Anyways. Getting back to Mum. There I was, stumbling along, trying to get to the finish line. The closer I got, the greater the pain. Not only my legs but my arms and feet; it was like every nerve ending in my body was now punishing my brain for tricking them into running so far. But I cou d not stop. Three thousand was waiting for Hillary; I would not be anyone's clown. Step by step, now walking like some sidestepping robot, I kept going towards where the finish tape had broken two hours earlier. For the last fifty feet, I could not feel most of my body as I dragged my limp left leg over the line and collapsed. The white light appeared in my head as I gasped for breath. I remember thinking I can go now; I have done my job. I felt a mask being put over my face and a familiar English accent say, I got you; it is ok, Adam, I am here. On opening my eyes, I could see my angel was back, but this time, she was wearing a red cross uniform."

"That moment, I held onto her arm and thanked Hillary for sending her back to me."

"I have never let go of her arm since, and I do not think I ever will.

A Time for Lepralites

A Time for Lepralites

1. New Beginnings

The wind howled, encircling his little hairy winged body.

"Titch-Ella," he roars weakly, but the blizzard drowns out his little voice.

On and on he flew, flapping his light wings through the bitterly cutting wind. He was losing, driven back by what felt like giant snowballs battering him. Through the howling noise, he thought he heard his friend.

Then.

WHACK!

Another sharp gust of wind twisted him upside down and slammed him into something sharp, like moving barbed wire from some scary movie, the tightening briars wrapped around his tiny body, impaling the creature in a netted trap.

He was overwhelmed by pain and numbness as he fell unconscious, hanging in the darkness.

****

The morning brought an eeriness.

The lack of wind left the countryside in a state of rest with its views showing a white snow blanket that laid over the countryside. It was rare weather for Southern Ireland. There must be something in the air that brought the winds of change not only in the climate's behaviour but also in the upheaval of families finding new ways of working. The pandemic could be blamed, or it was the sudden shift of thinking that allowed technology to become more prevalent in everyone's daily activities. Either way, it left most finding a new normal in their everyday lives.

This year had been a strange one in many ways for the McCarthy family too. It had brought many changes forced on them by the ongoing health issues of their youngest child, Clive, who over the last three years had many overnight hospital stays that left him hooked up to breathing ventilators. The doctors strongly recommended that he needed to live where the air was cleaner. It was a huge decision for the family but with the child's health getting worse they felt they had no other choice other than to act on the doctor's advice. His Mum and Dad moved swiftly to come up with a plan to move away from the city, but like most things, it was easier said than done. Aside from selling their townhouse, Katie, their daughter, who had built up her neighbourhood friendships, when she heard her parents telling her of the pending move there were many days of tears and tantrums. She knew it was for all the right reasons, however it was going to drastically change her life, and she had little control over the circumstances. The two girls whom she had known since she was a baby, who she had gone to preschool with, who sat next to her in class, who played in her house every second day, they would simply disappear from her life, despite her Mum saying they would try to visit them in the city, or her friends could come up and stay whenever they chose. It did not ease the pain of losing her buddies.

Being only seven years old, Clive was at an age where his friendships had not yet developed to the levels of sisters had. He was more concerned about what toys he could bring, especially the tank engines and carriages he had collected along with the tracks which Adam had put together in his bedroom. Many times, he checked with his parents to make sure they could disassemble and reassemble in the new house wherever that was going to be.

His Mum, Jane, was lucky enough that she was already working part-time from home, and as long as there was an internet connection with some way decent broadband, then she could keep doing her online support job in the health sector. For his Dad, Adam, finding a country-based retail management job was more challenging especially as many shops had found the previous year's difficult with many shoppers having turned to shopping online. As Adam had got older, the less he wanted to drive. As he had no wish to be driving in from the country every day, he was searching for the right job in the right place. The Gods were smiling on him, and he secured a store management position in the local co-op store.

Even though they thought it would take some time to sell their city townhouse, it sold quicker than they imagined, leaving them little time to find a home that would suit the family. With a restricted budget, they did manage to buy an old two-story cottage that would work for the family, even though it needed quite a bit of tender loving care to make it into a comfortable home. Now that their jobs and home were secure, there was just one giant, disorganised push to pack up their townhouse and move everything fifty-four kilometers up the road to North Cork and pile everything into their new place, which now felt more like living in a campsite than a home. Still, it was a great place to start their life's adventures in the countryside.

Still feeling the effects of the pulling and dragging of furniture and clothes and toys a few days earlier, Adam relaxed while sitting on the country-styled lounge window seat after getting up early to take some time to reflect on things as he often did. The house had a cosy feel to it. The embers were still smoldering in the stove giving out a warm feeling to the home on this bitterly cold morning. It was a massive change for Adam and Jane, who had both grown up in cities and knew nothing about living in the country. They always had big shops, bars, restaurants, and a lively nightlife with bustling streets within walking distance of their houses. In their town house they had to close their blinds and curtains when they slept to shut out the streetlight's invasion of their darkness. It sure was a different world from where they were living now. However, the shops were only a few minutes' drive from their new home, one of a cluster of six hillside houses overlooking the village in the valley. Each stone cottage had its own unique style. In the summer, I am sure it would all be idyllic. But now, for the McCarthys, it felt like a bleak stranded island, which was cut off from civilisation by the weather, where even the cars could not find the roads, not to mind drive on them. If it were a country that was used to getting plenty of snow, the cars would have chains on their wheels to grip the snow and ice. But Ireland was just not used to this stuff. Now, if it was rain we were talking about, that would be different, as everyone in Ireland had two umbrellas and plenty of waterproofs at the ready to use, on hearing the predictable soft rain forecasted.

But today, the family were all stuck indoors in a house on top of a snow hill as Adam looked out across the cambered hills of white. Although the McCarthys had two children, Katie, who was eleven, and Clive, just turning seven, it was Cody, their Shih Tzu dog, who took most of the looking after, especially during their city walkie times where he walked with his nose stuck to the footpath. When it came to traffic, he didn't have a clue. He had often stepped out onto busy roads and had to be pulled back to safety by the short lead the family used. They dare not leave him on his own, and his coat grew faster and thicker than any sheep. He was just one of these dogs that demands much attention in every way. And that included toilet time. Or, as the McCarthys had named it, pee pee time. Because seemingly, little dogs have little bladders, and he can never hold it for long. It was very much a case of "little and often" for Cody. This winter morning was no different as now he was scratching at the front door.

"Let me out. Let me out!"

As for Adam, dear old Dad, it was always a case of stopping what he was doing to leave the dog out in the garden. But this morning, because of a new house with an overgrown back garden and the side gate missing, Adam had to put on his welly boots, warm hat, and coat, and clipping the lead onto Cody's collar out they went. On stepping outside, he at once felt the snow underfoot, and not used to it, he walked carefully down what should have been his garden path and onto the road. Being from the city, the countryside felt deathly quiet to him. It was only eight o'clock; the winter sun had not risen properly yet. There were no cars or people around. He did not see the sense of having his dog on the lead. So, he unclipped it to allow him to run ahead. Even Cody could not get knocked down here.

"Wow, it sure is cold," he thought as he carefully chose his footing along the country road. Cody had no experience with this white phenomenon, as he tentatively jumped through it with some enthusiasm. He even tried to eat some. As his excitement grew with his confidence, he began zig zagging all over the road. As he ran ahead, Adam followed, using more of his time to reflect on the chaos of their last few days of moving vans and disruption. He began again to think about the changes it brought to the children's lives, Katie more so. On they walked, allowing his dog the freedom to get further ahead. He saw Cody turn into what looked like an old farmyard entrance. The dog started to bark, but he could not see him. His light brown and white colouring would make for good camouflage, especially in this snow. He could hear his dog upping the tempo with his growling and barking, which caused Adam to speed up. Now, walking quickly towards the noise, he rounded the corner. There he was. Cody. With his little stubby tail straight back and growling into the bushes. He pulled him back in case it was a wild badger or another animal that may hurt his pet. But he could not see anything at first. Then, down low where the bushes met the snow-patched grass verge, he thought he saw something move. It looked like an injured bird. Taking a handkerchief from his pocket, he carefully reached down under the bushes.

"There now," he whispered, "don't be nervous. What happened you little one?"

His voice trembled nervously. But it could have been the cold. He was worried for the little bird's health. Or was it a bird or some little doll that his daughter Katie might have played with when she was younger? But it was small. "Yes, maybe it's just a doll," he thought as he pulled it from the undergrowth; he could see it had blond plaited hair. He began to feel silly for picking rubbish from the ditch, especially on such an cy morning.

"What is this?" he thought. "It isn't a bird or a doll, and it seems alive." Carefully, he held it in his handkerchief. Then, from nowhere, he heard a quiet but high-pitched squeaky voice say,

"Is she alive?"

Cody began to bark wildly, looking up towards the top of the ditch. Adam forgot for a moment about his handkerchief

"It's me," the voice squeaked again, shrieking. "Up here. Is she okay?"

Confused between an unfamiliar voice, dog barking, and the cold in his ears, Adam looked down at the object in his hand. But it was neither a doll nor a bird. He had never seen anything like it. Long blond hair lay across a little chubby, unusual face covered in wet brown fur or hair. Its nose was flattened and broader than any human's. The mouth was shaped neatly, and its eyes were closed. Not wearing his glasses, he raised it towards his face to look closer. He could hear a very faint moaning noise. But it was not moving.

"The cold must be going to my head. I'm going nuts," he thought as he wrapped the handkerchief around it and pushed it down slowly into his coat pocket. He then turned his attention back towards the ditch. He saw two bright yellow eyes looking out from amongst the thorny hedging. But he could not see all the objects.

"I'm stuck."

"Be quiet, Cody," Adam grunted.

But the dog could not be silenced. With two hands, he reached deep into the whitethorn bush; the spikey thorns scratched his skin as he pushed the branches apart. There it was, whatever it was?

"Was it a huge butterfly?" he wondered, seeing so many colours before him.

"Maybe there are butterflies in the winter?"

 Trying to calm down his ridiculous thinking, he muttered to himself, "Shut up, Adam."

It was all getting too much for him to make logic of. It was another little animal with blue spiked hair, that sat on its head like a clump of grass. It was broader than the other. Its fur was greyer in colour. He could see its long arms wedged in the old growth of thorny sticks.

"Is she alive? Is she okay?" the little animal kept asking in a troubled voice.

"I don't know," he replied, not thinking much about what he was talking to. He continued to unwrap the strand-like thorny branches away from it. Suddenly, its arms were free, and it began to flap like a bird, but it could not move.

"I'm still stuck."

"It's my kilt; it snagged."

"Shut up, Cody," Adam raised his voice, stressing at the situation he had found himself in.

"Sorry," he found himself apologising to the little animal in the bushes. Finally, he pulled the last branch out of the way. The animal popped out and tried to fly. But it just fell onto the snowy ground, looked up at Adam for a moment then it fell unconscious.

Adam bent down and picked it up. He had no handkerchief left, so he placed it carefully into the other coat pocket. Cody was restless, sniffing around him as they quickly walked back toward the house. Adams's caution on the icy road had vanished, replaced only by his need to get home. He felt a strange calmness. He questioned himself, considering the mayhem he had just gone through, as he swiftly stepped towards home, muttering to himself trying to choose words to use in a sentence to explain these very different animals to his family. He hoped these things weren't dangerous or carrying a disease, but he felt good about rescuing them. Whatever they were? Now, Adam's brain was doing some zigzagging all over the place, just like Cody's walking patterns were.

"Who's a good boy?" Adam said to the dog, feeling guilty for shouting at him.

After all, Cody was the one who had found them.

"You sure are a good doggie," Adam struggled to open the old front door.

"Come on, Cody."

He walked towards the back of the house; his dog was still sniffing and growling. He waited until Cody was in the kitchen, then closed the door on him. Not a good idea! It was like an alarm going off. The dog had gone ballistic after being locked in. Adam's wife hurried from the front room.

"What on earth is going on? He will wake the children."

But before she could finish her sentence, a sleepy figure came down the stairs, rubbing the sleep from her eyes,

"What is wrong with Cody?" Katie asked with her tossed rumpled hair and pyjamas hanging loosely from her.

Adam ushered the ladies towards the front room, leaving Cody still mouthing off.

"I have a surprise," he stuttered.

Katie began to wake up at the thought of something nice coming her way, but Mum, on the other hand, was far more cautious as she thought her husband was acting strangely.

"What's up?" She enquired.

"Here, sit. I need to show you something."

"What?" his wife asked, showing no sign of taking a seat,

"I don't know," he replied, "But I think they might be qu te wonderful."

"What are you talking about?" Mum asked.

Trying to contain his excitement, he steadied himself. Slowly reaching into his pocket, his daughter's eyes followed his hands as he pulled out the little blue-haired animal. He semi clasped his hands, one over the other, treating it like a tender piece of gold silk between them which was about to blow away. As Mum and Katie moved in for a closer look, still with care, he opened his hands, keeping them semi-cupped in case the animal would fall to the floor. Gently, Katie rubbed the light, spiky blue hair with her forefinger. The little animal barely opened his eyelids to reveal its dim yellow glow. The little animal began to vibrate in Adam's hands.

"Oh, you poor thing," he said. "It is all wet and cold. Do we have a tea towel or something to keep him warm? He is shivering."

Adams concern grew, but Mum defenses were up, as she stepped back feeling some anguish of the unknown.

"We can't keep that thing in the house," she exclaimed.

But Katie was much more enthusiastic and ran to the corner of the room and pulled out a little doll's blanket from the pile of unstacked cloths and toys. With a bit of rummaging, she then lifted an old shoe box off the floor. She turned it over, leaving her little old dolls and bits and pieces she had previously packed, to fall onto the old, carpeted floor.

"We can use this," she said eagerly.

Not liking the situation but at the same time wanting to keep her daughter happy, Mum opened her hands for Katie to hand over the box. Adam slowly laid the animal onto the blanket, leaving Katie to wrap it carefully as she hugged it gently.

"That's not all," Adam said, reaching into his other pocket he pulled the little skinny blond-haired animal and his handkerchief, he opened the flaps back revealing the doll like figure,

"I think this one is badly injured. It has not moved since I found them."

Mum looked at Adams' open handkerchief, where she saw a doll-like creature lying across it like a limp rope; its helpless vulnerability grabbed Mums heartstrings.

Suddenly, she felt a need to help instead of fearing it.

"Oh, my word," she said, "we need to warm her up. Give me a moment."

She quickly ran upstairs and came back down with a soft face towel. Folding it carefully, she laid it into the shoe box. She slowly placed the little blond animal onto the towel. Then Katie followed suit, putting in the other one and covered them over with the doll's blanket. Mum set the shoe box down near the warm stove.

"They spoke to me. The blue one, I mean. It talked to me."

Adam knew he sounded off, but it was the truth.

"Are you losing your marbles? Did you hit your head out there?" Mum remarked, trying to get him to change the strange statement that he had just made in front of their daughter.

"Please listen," Adam insisted and continued with his excitement. "Katie, did you feel anything when you held the little animal?"

"Yes, I felt happy and peaceful but a bit strange."

She shrugged her shoulders.

"See. I told you." He was expecting his wife to see what he knew, but she did not.

"They are not ordinary animals. I will give you that." Mum joked at him skeptically.

"Yes, I know," he replied, "I know there is something special about these."

Still trying to brush the strange conversation aside, Mum said,

"OK. But for now, we will leave them to get warm and rest."

"Can I stay with them?" Katie asked.

"Of course," her parents agreed. "Just keep Cody away from them until we learn more about these animals."

They closed the door, leaving Katie to babysit the two little patients. Lowering her voice, Mum asked,

"Adam, will you go out into the shed and get Cody's old cage. Let's keep them in it; I don't want them moving around the house until we know what they are and where they come from? That is if they live? We have no idea what they are, not to mind how we are to look after them."

Adam agreed with his wife's caution and went outside to rummage in the shed looking for the old cage which he knew he had tossed in there during the home move frenzy.

****

2. Bedding in

I *don't know much about the psychology of dogs or how most dogs think.*

But I do know Cody.

****

Though he did not look very clever, he was a huge worrier. His childhood was relatively normal as dogs go. But for him, he was the last of five pups to be born, with two already left having not survived a young mother's birthing. The dog breeders were also expecting little Cody to leave too. He was what the breeders called the weakling or runt of the litter. When it came to feeding, if the breeder were not there to move the larger pups out of the way to allow him to get to the milk, then he would not drink. And later, when they moved to baby solids the other pups used to stampede over him to get to the food first. Not only did he get used to going hungry but because he was a lot smaller than the others, he was isolated. By the time Mum came to choose a pup there was only one left, Yes Cody. When she saw him, she was unsure whether she wanted him or not, as he looked so sickly. The dog breeder offered her the pup for half price, so she took him, knowing that she had the medical experience and the time to look after him. But it was the love for the dog that healed him, as the whole family fell in love with him from the moment, he was introduced to them. With Clive being the sickly one in the McCarthy family, it made sense that they would grow towards each other, and that is exactly what happened. Now it is hard to separate the two of them. During the times when young Clive is finding it hard to breathe in the middle of the night, it is Cody who jumps off their bed and runs barking to wake Mum and Adam. The little weakling had grown into an alert dog, and being the worrier that he is, had saved his friend on many occasions.

But tonight, while Clive, along with the rest of his family slept, he had only two things on his mind. And they were locked away from him in the front room.

"What were they up to in there?"

From the moment Cody saw them in the ditch he didn't trust them. And first impressions last. To him, they looked very dodgy and now they were staying in his house. So instead of sleeping at the end of Clive's bed, he decided that tonight he would stand guard, to ensure that they do not escape or cause harm to his family. He crept quietly down the stairs and sat down outside the living room door.

"Nothing will get past me now."

Even though he did not like many of the noises from the old house, like rattling letter box flaps, creaking timbers, and doors, at least he knew what was making the noise. But it was the not knowing anything about these new things? In his mind, it was pure silliness by the McCarthys to bring them into the house when they knew nothing about them. So, if he had to save his family from themselves and their thinking, that is what he would do.

Katie was up earlier than usual, worried about her new guests' health and wanting to know more about these strange creatures. Her thoughts were excited at the fact that the animals could talk. Or her Dad's imagination was telling the rest of the family a great story? But surely not, as he never had a great imagination. She came bounding down the stairs with anticipation of what the day might bring. On getting to the living room door, she had to step over their sleeping dog. Entering the dark, disorganised room, she closed the door slowly, not wanting to disturb any of the animals, but absent-mindedly, her hand turned on the light. There was a moment when she caught the end of a little blue animal jumping in under the doll's blanket.

She knelt beside the cage full of wonderment and whispered, "I know you are awake. I saw you."

She was shocked when a voice replied, "No, I'm not."

Her Dad had not dreamt it! They could talk.

"Wow," she thought and continued.

"Oh, don't be silly. I saw you jump in under the blanket."

"No, you didn't. I was too fast."

"My name is Katie," she spoke kindly, trustingly. "Can you talk to me?"

"I am talking to you," the voice replied.

"Now! Can you come out of your hiding place and talk to me?"

Slowly, his spiky blue hair and two yellow eyes appeared from under the blanket as it was pulled back.

"I'm Hoaby," he said.

She could see his chubby grey hairy cheeks and strange flat nose.

"Are you ok?"

She watched as the little thing stood up. It was not very big, only slightly taller than a robin. She was excited that the creatures could talk. His long, hairy arms draped down to his knees with three long fingers, and what looked like a skirt made from scale-like feathers hung from his waist. She noticed it had only three toes at the end of his oversized flat feet as it got closer. It grabbed the side of the cage. Doing so revealed what looked like a wing when he lifted his arm to hold the cage bars. It was the strangest thing Katie had ever seen or read about.

"Are you ok?" she repeated in her soft voice. "We were so worried about both of you. Is your friend, ok?"

The creature looked back into the shoe box. "I hope so."

Then he paused a moment.

"Why are we here? Why are we locked up in this cage?"

"Mum thought it was safer in case Cody would hurt you."

"Who is Cody?"

"He is our little dog."

"Yes. I met him. The noisy one!"

"Yes," she replied, "but he is a good doggie."

"He did not look like that to me."

"It was Cody who found you both in the ditch."

Katie was looking for some positives to show that Cody is not all bad while also hoping that they might end up as friends. But that was not going to happen today as the creature did not wish to speak of the dog. It was clear that the dog, too, had made a wrong first impression on the new house guest.

"Can I have water? I am thirsty," he asked in a husky voice, trying to clear his throat.

"Of course, I will get some straight away," she said, trying to please him.

She hopped up and went to the kitchen. The guard dog was still asleep on the floor. So again, Katie had to jump over him. It did not take her long to return from the kitchen with a small bowl full. Carefully, she opened the cage and slid it inside. Hoaby immediately went and drank from it.

"Poor thing," she thought. "He must be dehydrated."

"Yuck! What's that?" he jumped back away from the bowl. Katie was shocked at his reaction.

"That's horrible," the little one said, spitting it out from his mouth.

"It's water. You asked for water."

Katie was confused by his behaviour.

"That's not water. That's yucky."

Katie felt a bit insulted by his lack of gratitude. She got up and huffed, flicking her hair back indignantly.

"Well, that is all we have."

She turned off the light, stepped back over the dog again, and closed the door firmly. She felt annoyed with herself, even muttering like her Dad would do, when things got too much for him, even being angry with the poor dog asking him sarcastically, "Cody, are you on sleeping pills or something?" Still trying to understand what she did that was so wrong to the little thing.

"Or maybe that thing has a cranky mood because they had been locked in a cage? Or maybe it's me? Maybe the whole moving house thing has me this way? Maybe I should return to it and say I am sorry for losing my temper? Yes, that is what I will do," she thought.

Her mind was spinning.

As she turned, about to go back,

Whoops!

Either the door closing, or her muttering must have woken the dog, who was now back sniffing. Being careful to keep him on the outside, she slipped back through the half-held door in case he would try to nip past her.

"I am sorry, little one." She said in a meaningful voice, speaking straight from her heart.

"No, I am sorry," Hoaby replied. "But we cannot drink your tap water. There are too many additives put in it, and all the nutrients have been removed. It is not alive for us."

She was curious why simple tap water had upset him so much. "Why do you say that?"

"Our Elders taught us how humans pump all the good water into filters. Then, many chemicals are added to kill all the germs they believe will hurt them. So, by the time it gets to the tap, they have killed all its goodness, too. It is lifeless."

She switched subjects and was curious about where her caged creature had come from.

Katie asked, "What do you mean Elders?" Are there more of you?"

Hoaby smiled.

"Of course. Now. Who's being silly?" He began to joke with her.

"Where do you come from?" she asked.

"Up there," he pointed towards the back window facing up towards the forested area.

"I've never seen any of you before," she said.

"Well, that is not my fault," Hoaby replied, "maybe you weren't looking. You will never find what you are not looking for, you know!"

Already, Katie had become surprisingly relaxed that

something so small and hairy was talking to her, even though she was confused by its logic. In fairness, who would look for a furry animal with blue hair, yellow eyes, and wings that talks?

"Why are you here?" she asked cautiously.

"Because we are locked in a cage and can't get out," he replied.

It was clear she had asked very defined questions and was being rewarded with very defined answers, so she reworded her question.

"Why were you stuck in a bush on a cold winter morning?"

"The wind and the King of Ice pushed us into the ditch, and we got stuck. It was so sore. The long thorns hurt, and they tied me up, and I was so worried about Titch-Ella because I could not see her."

"Titch-Ella?" Katie asks.

"Yes. That's her name."

"How is she now?" Katie asked.

"She is sleeping, but she needs water, too."

"Oh, I am sorry. I will get you some real water."

She thought for a while about where she would find their natural water. Everything was still frozen! Then she had an idea. She got another bowl from the kitchen and went outside to the overgrown garden. She scooped snow from the large bushes and brought it back inside. Cody was still sniffing and growling at the door as she again pushed him away. She pushed the new bowl full of snow into the cage and took out the old one. Hoaby lifted some into his hand, pulled back the doll's blanket, and laid the snow on his friend's lips. In Katie's eyes, she looked so beautiful with her curly blond hair and light brown facial hair as she lay there like a sleeping beauty. The snow began to melt, bringing life back to her like she had been sprinkled with fairy dust.

"She must be a girl," Katie thought out loud.

Hoaby smiled. "Yes, she is. Just like you." Katie was entranced by how pretty she was, even though she looked a bit strange. Hoaby went back and sucked some snow himself.

"Thank you, Katie. That is much better now," he said as his eyes lit up to a brighter yellow glow.

"What are you? Are you Leprechauns?" she asked.

"No, although our Elders said we could have evolved from them. But I don't think so.

"Yes," she said. "I know what you mean. Some people say we have evolved from monkeys. But I don't think so either?" she thought momentarily, then asked, "Are you the fairies?"

"NO! Absolutely not." Hoaby looked horrified to be associated with fairies. "We are Lepralites. We have been around for ages."

By now, Cody was in a terrible state and could no longer hold back his barking. After hearing noise from inside the room, he repeatedly alerted Adam and his Mum of the danger Katie could be in. In Cody's head, Katie had no idea how dangerous these strangers could be. So, he had to take control of the situation. Adam came running down the stairs, tying the cord of his dressing gown. The two patches of grey hair on either side of his bald head remained uncombed. Half tripping on a step did not improve his poor mood.

"What in Lord's name are you barking at, ya clown? Cut it out."

Poor Cody, once again, had upset Adam. Even though he was doing his best to alert the family of the dangers, he got dragged out through the kitchen by the collar and put outside the back door very impatiently, even though there still was no side gate.

"Now. That will cool you off," Adam said, closing the door behind his dog.

"Wow. That wasn't very mannerly of him," Cody thought, getting a shiver on the back of the neck as his paws found the ice. He quickly trotted to the nearest pee point, lifted his leg, ran back to the door, and started to bark again. He would not allow his family to treat him in such a way by letting him out in the cold. The dog knew if he annoyed Adam for long enough, he would be left back in. So off he went again, using his higher-pitched bark as he knew his family disliked it, as they constantly complained about how it cut into their brains. And that was precisely what happened. The door opened, and Cody came inside! But this time, he found himself stuck in the kitchen with the entrance to the hall firmly closed. But life was not so bad, as Adam had placed a nice chunk of nuts and meat in his bowl on the floor for him to enjoy.

Now thinking

"Aw. Adam must have recognised the good job I did sorting

out those two problems in the front room," as he started to munch into his breakfast.

With the self-satisfaction of a job well done, he felt even more relaxed as he heard Mum come down the stairs, knowing she had more logic in her brain than Adam and Katie, who had always thought the best in every animal they met. He knew Mum would not put up with messing from the new house guests.

It was going to be a good day. Ah, beef gravy and nuts.

"My favourite," he thought, chewing his tasty food happily.

Jane entered the front room, throwing back the curtains to reveal the sun climbing up from the country's horizon, melting the land of its white glaze.

"Morning everybody." She sounded a lot spritelier than Adam, who was still sitting on the side of the sofa trying to wake up, as his daughter was explaining to him that "these little things are called Lepralites, and this is Hoaby, and the one who is asleep is called Titch -Ella. She's a girl."

"That's a beautiful name. Where did she get that name?" Mum asked.

"From the Elders," Hoaby shouted up from the cage.

Mum was in awe as she heard the little guy talk. She found herself struggling to accept it as the norm but hid her dismay as she continued with her questions, of which she had so many.

"And Hoaby. That's an adorable name, too. Is your friend, ok?"

"Yes, I think so. She got a big bang on her head. If we get a bang that is big enough, it always makes us sleep," he replied in a very matter-of-fact way.

Mum smiled at how he spoke so assuredly, but the little thing's human traits still shell-shocked her.

Katie then explained the water and how bad it was for them, "and probably us too," she added, for he had made a lot of sense to her.

"Yes," her Mum agreed. "I could never understand the whole water thing either. It is all a bit of an overkill if you ask me. Sur didn't people all survive just fine on well water for years. And now we are all asked to buy pure water in a PLASTIC bottle! Makes no sense."

Hoaby listened and thought, "This lady is so clever for a

human." Usually, according to the Elders, humans were not expected to be so clever. The mere mention of plastics or plastic particles would make a Lepralite shiver with distaste. It was the worst thing the humans had come up with and humans just kept finding new stuff to make from it. If a Lepralite swallowed some plastic particles, it would cut their tummies to pieces as their main diet was leaves, seeds, and water. Their little body workings were too fragile for that.

Kate nodded. From listening to her Mum's logic and Hoaby's cutting explanations of why they hated and feared plastic so much, she declared, "Ok. Let's then make this house a plastic-free zone,"

"That will be hard," Adam stated. "Most of everything we buy in the shops is wrapped in plastic, even our fruits. Case in point: have a look around here."

He pointed around the room; and as Katie looked, she could count seven big plastic bags. Even her old dolls were plastic. She had never dwelled on this issue before, but now she could see how overwhelmed by plastic we all are. Even the babies, as she could see her brother's old toddler toys piled up in the corner waiting to be thrown out, and these were all made from plastic too.

"Yes, but we do need to try," she said. "A child's simple logic was always logical but sometimes hard to implement because of years of human mistakes being fixed by more mistakes!" her Mum added.

A light, hoarse voice came from the cage.

It was the little female Lepralite. Katie was captivated again, this time by her large, round, turquoise blue eyes, which exuded kindness but showed a sense of confusion.

"Why are we here, Hoaby?" she asked.

"It's ok, Titch. We are safe."

"I was so scared, Hoaby. I was sure we would wake up in Never Never Land."

"It's ok," Hoaby assured, holding her head, "The McCarthy's saved us. Mr. Adam took us out of the briars."

"What briars? I was just so cold and couldn't see you. I kept calling for you,"

She was baffled and was stumbling over her words.

"We are safe now. Take some more water here."

He lifted more snowy water, and she drank from his cupped hand. Everyone could see its benefit to her but also the kindness Hoaby was showing her. Titch-Ella looked around at her surroundings, trying to take it all in, but she could not, so she settled on the deep brown eyes full of care transfixed on her.

"Who are you?" she asked.

"I am Katie. My dog, Cody, and Adam, found you."

Titch -Ella felt quite dizzy, and her head hurt a lot.

"I think I got bumped."

"Yes, that is what Hoaby thought," Katie added.

"I need to rest a bit more," Titch-Ella said, lying down again.

Katie got up to follow her parents out of the room.

"Rest, you two. I will be back in a while. We will keep the

door closed so you will be safe."

****

"How are we going to escape Titch-Ella?" Hoaby whispered to his friend.

"I need to close my eyes and think about it."

Sometimes, the world needs to wait for us to get ourselves right.

3. No Photos Please

A cutting sound of scraping on glass woke Hoaby.

The late afternoon sun threw a shadow through the curtains, showing a huge tiger or lion outside. He began to shake Titch-Ella frantically.

"OH, Hoaby, please go back to sleep."

"Look, Look, it's a huge cat at the window; it's coming in."

The shadow moved back and forth across the sill. There was

a loud Miaow, a screeching cry and then again, another Miaow.

Then silence.

Hoaby's throat felt dry. He could feel his body tremble as his imagination took over. He started thinking of a huge animal ripping their cage to pieces, with no way for them to escape.

"Titch-Ella, wake up. There's something outside."

He listened as a door opened.

Then Adams voice said" go get them" followed by Cody's rasping barking, the bushes rattled, and a loud screech cut the air as the predator left the garden. Cody stood at the edge of the overgrown garden with his tail up and legs planted firmly on the wet ground. He meant business. He was growling, making it clear to his family that he was collecting some brownie points.

"If that cat thinks he can come and go as it pleases, he has another thing coming? I'm the boss around here."

"Good boy, Cody," Adam said as his dog pranced back into the kitchen, carrying his ego with pride.

"It's okay, Titch-Ella. The dog scared it away," Hoaby said with relief.

"Maybe the dog is handy to have around."

He pulled the blanket up around his friends' shoulder and tucked it around her, then lay down on the woolen cloth. She did not stir, she was in a deep sleep, where even Hoaby's voice could not reach.

A calling shout out sounding like distant ringing bells, "Diggerrr .... Diggerrr."

Repeatedly, the neighbour's voice rang out.

"This place is all a bit crazy," Hoaby thought. "Maybe Titch-Ella has the right idea." He laid back again and closed his eyes.

A new day dawns.

The little ones had slept for well over sixteen hours. when Hoaby opened his eyes to a vision of his angelic-looking friend standing over him. Seeing her blond curls hanging happily and her ocean-blue eyes shining through the morning gloom was an excellent sight for him to see. Her feathered-like kilt wings looked like they had just been renewed. He jumped up with enthusiasm for his day ahead. His mood had changed from a fearful one back to his cheerful self.

"Well, how are we going to get out of this place?" he asked. He expected Titch-Ella to have a plan, for she always had one, but she only replied, "We wait."

"We wait? That's not a good plan at all."

He could feel a sense of calmness in his friend, who seemed to know what she was doing.

"We need to just wait for the world to catch up with us and let things open up in their way."

He had no idea what she was talking about. But he accepted what she had said, as he had no plan.

Hoaby had always been different from Titch-Ella, as she had always been more philosophical. In contrast, he was a blatant reactionary who would only react to one situation at a time or give one answer at a time—not even trying to choose his words as he would spout out his version of the truth. He had no filters between his brain and mouth. She, however, always used her words carefully in case she hurt someone's feelings or wanted something that may take a bit of maneuvering of words to get what she wanted. In the animal kingdom, she would be what's known as a Wyley old fox. She always got what she needed between her clever thinking and angelic looks. However, it was never for herself. It was used to help her on one of many projects to help other animals or situations she thought needed her help.

The door opened.

It was Katie.

"Good morning, little ones."

She pulled back the curtains to allow the room to fill with light. She then knelt next to the cage.

"Well, you both look a lot better today. Would you like some more water? The snow has melted. But I am sure there are some pools I can find."

"Yes, please," Titch-Ella said.

"I'm starved," Hoaby interrupted in his usual impatient manner.

Katie smiled. "Of course, you must be. What do you guys eat?"

"Nuts, fruit, berries, seeds," Hoaby stating his desires.

"Ok, I will see what Mum has."

Again, closing the overused door, she returned to the kitchen where her Mum and Adam were trying to make sense of their new house by cleaning the cupboards.

"Do we have any seeds or fruit in the house? It's for the little ones."

Mum remembered her days in the city when she be-friended a little robin who had injured itself in their back garden.

"I think I know what they will eat," she said with a smile. Taking a cutting from a loaf of home-baked brown bread, Mum smeared a thick, fruity layer of strawberry jam over it, then cut it into small cubes and put them on a little plate. She licked the jam from her finger and said, "I think this will make their day."

Katie went back to the room.

"Mum thinks that you should like this."

Carefully opening the cage, Katie put in the plate full of food and removed the bowl. She did not like feeding her new friends this way; it felt like she was feeding a hamster, but she would not go against her parents' wishes. On leaving the little ones to eat, she searched outside for natural water in the garden but could not find any. What could she do? She returned to the kitchen, looking for her dad's help to solve their garden's water shortage. Her Dad had a Ding moment.

"Come with me." He placed her bowl under the rainwater downpipe.

"Now leave that for a few minutes."

Sure enough, the drips off the roof reached the bowl.

"If our friends are going to stay, we need to make a freshwater catchment to save water for them," Adam said, handing Katie a full bowl. "Just one more job that needs to be done around here," he muttered as Katie smiled, then kissed him on his cheek, rewarding him for his efforts, and then returned to her guests.

In the meantime, Hoaby had smelled the fresh bread and its topped fruity delightful jam and was impatiently munching on it with crumbs spraying all over the cage as he used his excited words.

"You need to taste this Titch-Ella." She cautiously lifted her piece towards her nose, smelled it, then took a nibble from a corner, saying,

"Yes, it's nice."

"No, you need to put it all together," Hoaby said; his words were excited, "It needs to all go in together."

So, opening her mouth, she followed Hoaby's instructions.

Then.

Boom!

She was hooked, as the taste rattled on her taste buds.

"MMMMM. That is gorgeous," she agreed.

After seeing the half-empty plate and the two guests focused entirely on their food, Katie sat on the floor next to the cage and said, "I think Mum got it right with your food."

Hoaby, still spraying crumbs, replied, "It's delicious."

" Yes, it's very lovely. Thank you, Katie." Titch-Ella said. Moving towards her, Titch-Ella continued.

"Can we get out of this cage? I need a stretch."

"I'm not sure. My parents said you need to stay in there to keep you safe." Katie stuttered, finding it hard to say no.

"We are safe in the house, aren't we?"

"Yes. But ...." Katie thought momentarily as if she did have a point.

"Please," Titch-Ella asked again. "We will die if we are kept here too long as we must fly." Katie understood exactly how she felt, as she had the same feelings when she ended up grounded for doing something her parents had told her not to do. She could still remember what it was like having to stay in her room without access to her phone or laptop and the whole world on the outside waiting for her. It was terrible.

"OK," Katie said casually, then paused." But only if you promise to return when I ask you to."

Katie unlocked the catch on the cage door, and Hoaby at once skipped out like Jack Flash in a hurry, jumping into the air. He opened his arms, showing off his grey wings. His array of blue and yellow feathered kilts fluttered as he glided across the living room air and straight into the back of the sofa.

BUMP!

He dropped to the floor.

"Are you ok, Hoaby?" Katie got a fright. But he reappeared

from behind the couch into full flight again; he glided over and landed on the top of the TV. He flapped and straightened out his wings. He noticed Katie looking at him.

"I'm fine. Who put that silly thing there? I could have hurt myself."

"That's our Hoaby," Titch-Ella puffed out her little cheeks, smiling. "He has been practicing flying for over four years but is getting better."

"Yes, a lot better," Hoaby declared. "I hardly crash anymore."

Katie smiled as she listened to her two little friends have a banter. Katie enjoyed their innocent humour. Titch-Ella leapt up, and with widened, gracious, shaded red wings, she flew from the cage with natural ease. Higher she flew, gliding and weaving around the room around the furniture, then down under the coffee table and up again until she rested on top of the curtain pole. Her beauty in flight amazed Katie as she flew more gracefully and with more agility than anything she had ever seen.

Katie's peaceful, happy thoughts were rudely interrupted by the door swinging open, and a small boy came plodding in, holding a toy soldier doll in his hand. And yes, you guessed it, the boy's best buddy, Cody, came running in with frenzied excitement, barking wildly up at the TV. Panicking, Hoaby flew quickly up to sit next to Titch-Ella. Katie tried to grab hold of the dog. But he was too quick, skittishly hopping about the room. It was easy to see that he wished to be set free to alert Mum and Adam of the animal's escape, for still in the dog's head, they were threatening Katie. Adam rushed into the room, grabbed Cody, and lifted him off the floor.

Katie felt rushed as she tried to introduce her little brother to the Lepralites,

" This is Clive, my baby brother," but they could only wave down at the boy and say "Hi" as Cody had everybody's full attention,

"Calm down. Shush. Will you calm down!"

Adam rubbed Cody's head, who now thought he needed to listen to his master, so he quietened, leaving only a few light growls and whimpers. Then the other boss appeared.

It was Mum.

"What the blazes is going on in here?"

Her sharpened voice pierced the room,

"Whoops," thought Titch-Ella. "We are in for it now."

"Katie McCarthy. Did I not say they were to stay in the cage?"

Katie dropped her head and muttered, "They needed to exercise."

Adam agreed that they did need some exercise. He was the one who always tried to ease the family's friction.

"We are sorry. We mean no harm," Titch-Ella said. "We only needed to stretch our wings, and Katie helped us. It was all my fault."

"Well ...." Mum paused, stopping herself from giving out anymore. She could hardly believe what she heard; a small animal was apologising and taking the blame.

"Who are these things?" she thought.

She was astounded by their human nature, or was it just nature? She questioned herself. She knew there was a trusting calmness about these agile creatures, and even though they were very different from anything else she had ever met, they gave her a feeling that, somehow, she could trust them. She came from a family that was always made feel different, having grown up in an extraordinary society and having parents of different colours and from other parts of the world. Many humans strangely had hurtful opinions about her Mum and Dad being together—such crazy times. But little Jane had to grow up and learn from a young age that she needed to build a bubble around her and her family. Many years later, when she came to Ireland and met Adam, she removed some of that protective bubble. But now, Mum felt she needed to build that bubble back, this time around her vulnerable little house guests, for she was afraid to let anybody see them as they could try making a show of the little ones, making them out to be freaks or sticking them in a circus cage for customers to jeer at. The more she thought of such, the more frightened she became for them; how could these little creatures protect themselves against this pitiful element of society?

"Thank you so much for that yummy food. It was so delicious," Hoaby shouted down from the curtain rail, looking towards Mum.

"Fairies, Fairies," Clive said, pointing up at them.

"We are not fairies," Hoaby shouted back.

"Fairies, Fairies. I see fairies. Look Dad."

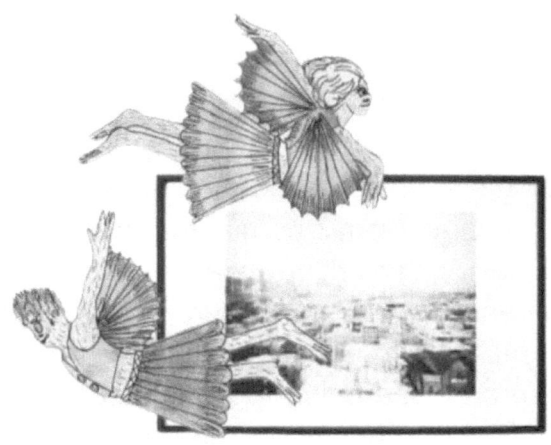

Adam put Cody back on the ground, telling him to "sit" and "shut" in a stern-mannered voice, then lovingly picked up his child.

"They are Lepralites." Changing his tone to converse with his son's young age.

"They are small, tiny," Clive insisted.

"You're small, Hoaby shouted back.

"NO! I'm a big boy," Clive wailed back.

"Oh. Calm down the pair of you," Adam said, "Come on, boys - we will go for a walk." He put Clive down again and held Cody's collar, bringing them outside to the hall, preparing for a walk, boots, coats, lead, and then the door closed.

The dull winter's day gave hope that the snow had left, and the rain was waiting overhead all bottled up in dark grey clouds which at any moment could decide to lose its load on

North Cork once again. But for now, the quiet boreens that ran past their cottage was a great place for the dog to run and Clive to chase. Or sometimes even the other way around!

But either way Adam had time to relax a bit when they were keeping each other busy. It was the first time he stood still on the road leaving his eyes follow the lines of the fields down towards the market town in the valley. The white snow clumps cleared quickly with the warming temperatures and of course the very soft rain showers. Once again, the dog passed him by. It was nice to see his dog run free instead of always being restricted by a lead as he had been in the city. Clive was next to run on past still calling Cody to wait. Adam began to feel joyful freedom as he looked at the views around him. Or maybe it was the fact that his child was running without wheezing and coughing as much as he used to,

"Yes, I am so happy to be here" he said out loud as though he was thanking God or the universe for bringing him to live on this patch of land with sweet clean air and wonderful views and most of all an amazing family. And yes, two very strange house guests. At that point Cody jumped up on him looking for his attention, Adam leaned over, picked him up and said, "Yes my boy, you are a part of our family too." Then he put him down again to run with Clive.

Mum sat back into the oversized chair to rest, trying to absorb and adapt to what felt like the new normal that had come to her house. It was all such a strange feeling. But she felt relaxed and safe in her new environment, even enjoying her new very disorganised home and their new guests.

Thinking and choosing her words carefully, Mum said, "Titch-Ella, that's a beautiful name and very rare."

Again, pausing mid-sentence, "Do you know when I heard your name, I checked where it came from, and my research showed me it was the name of a lagoon in Australia—a beautiful place by all accounts. You were well-named, with your lagoon blue eyes and your skirt coloured red/yellow, like a desert. Who gave you your name?"

"Our wise Elders always give our names when they look at us. I don't know how they do this. They are old and wise."

"Ya," said Hoaby, "and we are young and unwise."

Mum smiled again at his simplicity.

"I searched for the Lepralites, and Google told me that you are a fictional character from the forest."

"Is Google your Elder?" Titch-Ella asked.

"No, it's a search engine on the World Wide Web on the computer that people use to find out about anything."

"So strange," Titch-Ella replied confused.

"It's not as good as our Elder if it thinks we are just fiction," Hoaby stated.

"Perhaps not Hoaby," Mum smiled.

"I have an idea," Katie said. "Can I take a picture of you? Then we can look up on Google Images and see if you are real."

"Ha, of course, we are real," Hoaby felt hurt by her silly comment.

"I meant to say real to the rest of the world. I mean…. oh, you know what I mean." Katie confused her words, trying to stop insulting the little ones. But her mouth was not following her brain, so she skipped the rest of her sentence and started flapping at her jeans' pockets with her hands as if trying to find something.

"Aw, there we go." She took her phone from her pocket and pointed it towards the curtain rail, briefly leaving it to focus. She clicked, and there was a slight flash.

"Now. That wasn't so hard then, was it?" she asked as she searched her phone's photo album.

"Now, Mum. Look." she said excitedly, looking at her snapped image.

"Oh no - it didn't come out. Maybe it was not focused."

Confused by the lack of a picture, Katie said.

"Can we do that again?"

She moved closer, tak ng her time to steady her hand.

She clicked again.

But again, the image just revealed what looked like a ball of fire sitting in the middle of the picture instead of two smiling Lepralites.

"Hoaby, this looks like you don't exist," she said, looking up at them.

"We never exist for cameras," Titch-Ella announced. "Maybe that is why humans have made us fiction."

"It's all extraordinary," Katie added.

"Maybe, but we aren't fiction!" Titch-Ella continued. "I don't know who Google is, but I know who we are and where we live, and our world is very real for us."

"I'm sure it is," Mum replied. "Maybe we need to start trusting each other?"

"Yes," Titch-Ella replied with her chubby-cheeked smile. "Trust is always a good start."

"Does that mean we don't need to stay in the cage?" Hoaby asked hopefully.

"Oh, I think we can trust you," Katie added. "Isn't that right, Mum?"

"Yes, but I think Cody will have a problem with that."

"Can you leave him to me? I will talk to him?" Titch-Ella asked.

Mum stood up and started to speak in an organised manner.

"OK, we will take the shoe box out of the cage and fold the pen. Now, where can we put your bed? What about the shelf over the TV? Yes, out of harm's way."

"Yes, that would be good." Thinking aloud, "There is room for the water bowl up there, too."

So that is where they would stay on the shelf over the TV. Safe from anything that could harm them. Mum still knew not to expect too much from wild animals as she already had the experience with the robin that broke her heart when it left despite her giving it a safe place to heal. With all her time and care, she even collected worms and fed the robin with seeds, watching it improve until it was able to fly again and get better. For a short time, it had stayed close to their garden after being set free, popping in occasionally to say hello. But then it stopped calling. She found a little hole forming in her heart. As time passed, the days turned to weeks, and that hole widened. She kept hoping her robin would come back and say hello, she started dreaming up some happy endings of the robin flying back to her, bringing her partner and some little chicks with it. But her dream did not come true. She had to accept that it met its mate and got on with life without her.

"The Lepralites will probably do the same when they are ready," she thought.

" But I will enjoy their delightful company if they decide to stay with us a bit longer. Life sure is about taking one day at a time."

****

4. Dressing the Tree

We are not putting that thing up again this year."

Poor Adam. He had just spent two hours digging in the jam-packed shed for the family Christmas tree, which they had used every year since they got married.

Sixteen years ago, when they bought the lavish tree, it was in vogue with its six-foot brown stem and green branches covered in glitter. It had been just the right size to fit their townhouse's front room. The years had brought many new things to hang on to, so much so that their memories weighed down the branches. Mum had spoken sternly enough to Adam for him to know that he would not get the old tree past her again this year. He was sorry to see it go, but he came to the consolation that he had saved a lot of money by not having to buy a different tree every year. He went over by the thrash, said goodbye to their old tree, snapped it in half, and stuffed it into the garbage bin. To an onlooker watching him depositing his old plastic Christmas tree into the bin, one might be forgiven for thinking that he is a heartless man. But far from it. For the last two years his wife wanted to change the tree, and each time the subject was broached, Adam would pull out the old Christmas photos that he had kept and most of them were taken around the tree keeping a lot of memories alive. The tree to him was like his handle to catch himself from falling. He found it hard to let go of old things. They seemed to give him security when he brought them with him to his present or future and the tree was just one more thing that was becoming his wife's nemesis. But no more.

New Home.

New Tree.

The End. And he had to accept it.

Titch-Ella was happy to see the old tree go. For the last few days, she had tried to explain to her new family why putting up a real tree was so important. Christmas time for Lepralites was about feeding their senses, such as love, joy, and happiness. Visually, with shiny ingots and lights, and with their heightened sense of smell allowed them to wallow in the happy smells of cakes and puddings. But most of all, the scent of pines and spruce woody Christmas trees. She knew the trees that the humans used for this time of year were grown especially for Christmas, as they would grow daffodils, roses, and lilies for other occasions. The humans sure did like to give lush-smelling flowers to each other. It didn't seem right to have a tree they could not smell.

That evening as Clive slept and Cody lay at the end of his bed, he began to hear a lot of rattling in the attic. At first, he thought it could be a mouse in the attic, but he remembered that when he was only a pup, the McCarthy's had found a mouse in their city house. This was a different sound. He was trying so hard to stay on the end of the bed and sleep. But as soon as he closed his eyes, there was another rattle. He knew if he started to alert the house, it would be himself who would get in trouble, for it was nighttime, and anytime he warned them when Adam was asleep, the result would be the same. The noise was over his head now and really beginning to annoy him. Then suddenly, there was a bang in the attic like something had dropped.

"Enough is enough," he thought as he jumped off the bed and ran out onto the landing. He barked wildly at the attic door. Suddenly, his collar was grabbed. Oh no, it was his Adam.

"What are you barking at? You will wake the house again. What's wrong with you?"

Cody felt his paws being dragged across the timber floors as he was pulled back into Clive's room, then he was lifted onto the bed, and a finger pointed at him.

"The next time you are out, Cody." Then the door closed. Cody whimpered in response to Adams' lack of understanding of the situation and laid his head back on the quilt.

"I bet our guests downstairs know what's going on?" He thought.

In the meantime, downstairs, Titch-Ella was shaking Hoaby.

"Can you hear that?"

"No," he replied. "Go to sleep."

"Hoaby, wake up. Can you not hear them?"

She persisted.

"No, I can only hear you now. GO to sleep."

He was getting cranky.

Giving up on looking for her friend's attention, she smiled, rolled over, tucking her hands under her little hairy face, and began looking forward to another adventure tomorrow.

Adam returned to his bed, thinking he needed to check out the roof the next day. The dog must have been barking at something, but he was too tired to investigate now. Maybe it was a loose slate allowing the wind into the attic; perhaps that upset the dog, he thought as he drifted back to his uneasy sleep, tossing and turning with a thousand thoughts running over his head. Eventually, he did get some sleep, but the morning arrived too soon for him, and he woke up later than the rest of the household. Adam came slowly down the stairs, only half awake. His pajamas felt twisted on him, reflecting the way he felt about life as he grumbled to himself about all the jobs he had yet to do today.

"Oh, you're in great form today," Mum said teasingly looking at the wall mirror while rubbing lipstick across her lips.

"That dog is doing my head in. Maybe it's the new house?" Adam declared. "Maybe it could be the wind in the attic? I will check it later."

"OK, but in the meantime, can you go and get dressed, as a Christmas tree is being delivered in a little while."

It was like music to Adam's ears, hearing that it would be delivered, as he dreaded having to bring one home from town on the roof of his car. He had conjured up pictures in his mind of a massive, big tree spread over the top of his little car, with its draped branches hanging down both sides, blocking his view while trying to drive, with all the towns' people laughing as he passed them by. Thank the Lord we don't have to do that, he thought. It didn't take long for him to transform from a moaning ogre to a smiling Adam.

"That must be them," he said.

Looking out from the bedroom window towards the village, he could see a tractor and trailer laden with trees, meandering its way up the narrow, winding road towards them. It took less than five minutes to arrive. The two young lads who had travelled on top of the trailer passed down the tree to Adam. It was easy to see they were well practiced in the art of tree offloading, with their care and efficiency, as they landed the tree safely down into his hands and were off again.

"The tree is perfect in every way, a bit plump perhaps, but it will do!" Adam thought as he watched the tractor move around the corner to drop more trees up to his neighbours. He could hear the children's anticipation build up inside the house, but he called for Mum's help to get the wide tree through the narrow cottage door. With a bit of effort and a lot of puffing and dragging, they managed to get it into the front room, where they were greeted with tremendous excitement from Cody wagging his tail along with Hoaby and Titch-Ella, who were bouncing across the furniture, awaiting the wonder of seeing their first tree in a human's house.

Titch-Ella had got her dream. She took a deep breath, inhaling all the wild, woody smells she had hoped for; her sense of smell brought feelings of forest freedom. Hoaby felt homesick, remembering his clan and their gatherings in the winter evenings, where the damp, grounded old tree foliage smelled as it softened underfoot. Hoaby's solitary moment did not last long as he was bowled over by Cody, who had run straight over him, being carried away by his happy doggy excitement after seeing his pal Clive come in the door. As always in the morning, he would jump up on the boy and give him morning licks and kisses. Cody had scant regard for anything that would get in his way during this ritual, not even a tiny Lepralite. Hoaby got up, shaking off the dog's clumsiness, and joined back in the joyful moment with Mum on her mission, getting the tree standing into an old bucket and wedging it in place using rocks and sand with Adam and Katie doing all the packing and running about as Mum held the tree in a vertical position. When done leaving the tree standing by itself, she stepped back, putting her hands on her hips, proud of the job so far.

Then Mum looked at the little ones and said, "I want to explain to you as we put up the tree what a real Christmas means to me."

"Can we put up the lights?" Katie asked Dad. But once they started, they found it difficult to wrap the flex around the tree's long branches; they had started at the bottom and tried to work to the top, but they were struggling. Katie looked towards the little ones who were perched on top of the back of the couch watching the family goings on,

"Can you guys help us please? We cannot wrap it as it's too wide and high." They did not have to be asked twice, for in a blink of an eye, the two Lepralites took hold of the electrical lead full of star lights and skipped their way up the tree branches, bringing the cable around and around to the top and then halfway back down again, before they ran out of lead.

Then Mum said. "These lights remind me of stars that guide us in our darkest nights." Opening a box full of neatly paper-wrapped glass baubles, she continued.

"The blue is the one we got when Clive was born. The pink was when Katie joined the family. The yellow and green are Adams and mine. The orange and white ones remind us of my parents, and the red and silver remind us of the Adams family. And these two glass ones with snowflakes are new."

She paused and looked at Titch-Ella and Hoaby.

"These glass baubles will always remind us of you two, whether you are near or far." Then, from the bottom of the box, Clive reached in and pulled out a big plastic bone covered in glitter, "Ah yes, this is Codys'," and she hung it on the tree with the same care as the fragile glass baubles.

Titch-Ella and Hoaby were overwhelmed by the love that had just been shown to them. But before they could say anything, Mum asked Clive to open the box of teddy bears. There were twelve different ones, all just slightly smaller than the Lepralites, one for each month of the year.

"When I look at these, they remind me of the months we have lived through since our last Christmas. I remember the good and bad times that we have worked through as we had journeyed through the last year."

Each teddy was placed carefully on different thick branches around the tree. Mum moved on to the next part,

"The trinket boxes. Each year, Adam gives me something to add to the tree. He handed me a plastic ring during the first year we were together. It was given with his wish that one day we could afford an expensive wedding ring for me.'

Then she pulled out a little pink shoe and hung it. "Adam gave me this when I was pregnant with our little Katie here. I always wondered how he knew a little girl would arrive."

Her memories brought smiles from her reflective thoughts as each piece was hung up. "Then there was a tiny bicycle he gave me when I was pregnant with Clive."

After thirteen more trinkets had been tied and were dangling from the tree, Adam had one more surprise as he handed Mum a little wrapped present. On opening it, she found a key with a small string attached.

"This is the key to our whole new life in the country."

She smiled and kissed his cheek, then hung it on the tree. By now, the tree was full, so Katie asked. "Can we make the star now?"

Mum replied. "of course, we have no star yet."

There was a tradition in the McCarthy household that the children made a new star every year. Katie knew the routine by now and said, "I will go and get a cereal box, scissors, tinfoil, glue, and sellotape."

"Good memory, Katie," her mom said. "But you forgot some things."

Katie looked blankly at her, searching for the answer.

"Ruler and pencil," Mum reminded her, and Katie ran upstairs in search of some of the required items before she searched the kitchen for the rest of the list.

Cody had seen his family were all in good spirits and had followed Katie up the stairs to finish his promised mission. Maybe now is a good time to remind Adam of the attic situation? He stood on the landing and started barking again, hoping the family would believe his alert. Even though there was no noise right now, he would not risk another night of noise from the attic.

"No rest for the wicked," Adam said, getting up from the chair he had just sat on.

"I am sure that dog has a problem with me resting. I had better check the attic. If I don't, we won't get much sleep tonight either."

He headed up the stairs carrying the stepladder with him.

Meanwhile, the children cut out the star and pasted the foil onto the cardboard shape. Suddenly, a scream came from upstairs, which stopped them all. They waited as they could hear Adam coming quickly back down.

BOOM, BOOM, BOOM!

Down the stairs into the front room, he was puffing and panicking, with a big red face that carried a bit of spider webbing that hung from his eyelashes.

"What's wrong?" Mum asked. "Are you OK?"

"It's bats. We have bats in our attic. I hate bats."

His drama had taken over.

"Oh, for goodness' sake," Mum said calmly. "They are only mice with wings. Go take them out."

"Not in your Nelley. I'm not going back up there until they are gone."

"OK, I will do it," Mum said, getting up from the floor where she had been instructing the children.

Titch-Ella asked. "May I go up and talk to them?"

But before Mum could answer, Adam jumped in, agreeing,

"That's a great idea. I can't. They could fly into the back of my head and get tangled in my hair. We have all heard the stories, you know."

Mum smiled at her husband's bald head but did not comment.

Titch-Ella started laughing as she knew what Mum was smiling at.

"What's wrong with you?" Adam huffed at her.

Thinking it was better to change the conversation away from what she was thinking, Titch-Ella replied,

"Don't be silly. Bats are too fast and too clever to crash into the back of anybody's head. And they are far too clever to get stuck in hair. Even yours, Mr. McCarthy!"

Mum and Katie started to giggle. Imagining a bat getting entangled in Adams's little bits of grey hair on his bald head would take a lot of imagination. Mum switched back the conversation" You two had better go up to the attic and see what's going on."

The little Lepralites skipped up the stairs. Then, they hopped and flapped into the tight, dark attic space. Their eyes began to glow brighter until they lit the extended, narrow area with blue and yellow eyes. Then they saw something they did not want to meet at the end of the attic. Hanging from the cross beams were Vargas and his son, Sisaroe. Why is he here? As they moved closer, she wondered if his dislike for humans had brought him here. Or maybe worse, was it a disaster after happening amongst their clan?

Vargas was the region's head honcho, big cheese, boss bat.

Titch-Ella knew well that this bat was not to be messed with. She could not understand why the boss bat had come in person all this way for them.

"Well, well, well. Look who it is. Our two lost little Lepralites."

Titch-Ella and Hoaby gasped. They knew they were in for a lecture. The bats had always protected the Lepralites so much so that they began to feel like they had adopted forever angry parents. The bat's laborious lectures would drain a swamp, not to mind two little Lepralites having to listen to them.

In the animal Kingdom, they are known as" wise heads on old necks."

They always take a cautious approach to life. Bats can see everything that could go wrong with any plan before anything was even started. So, their experiences with new items are minimal, as they stay well within their comfort zone. They rarely experienced anything new, as they would conclude the worst would befall them if they ever tried anything new. However, the Lepralites were the exact opposite. They would carry their optimistic heads on young shoulders. No matter what their plan, they assumed it would turn out just fine, which did not always happen. Case in point: the time our two little friends ended up stuck in a ditch, and if Cody had not found them, the game would have been up for them, and they would be in Never Neverland by now.

Vargas continued, "We warned you not to fly that evening, but as always, you did not listen."

His voice grew richer as he verbally began slapping down the little ones.

" I have been out looking for you both for some time now, putting myself and, of course, the other bats at risk flying in all sorts of weather. And where do we find you? Yes, IN A HUMAN'S HOUSE."

He was boiling over with anger, but Titch-Ella brazened it out. Looking up at his twisted, snarling face glaring down at her, he saw that his anger was not impacting her as he thought it might. He was expecting her to be cowering in a corner by now, as others would have shown more fear of his anger. He gathered himself and toned down his voice.

" I hope you both have learned to listen to my advice in the future, as I am usually right."

Of course, the lesson that should have been learned was to listen to the bats and take note of the weather before they flew. But it was always about the bat's ego, and they must always be correct.

"Now, come on, go back to the clan," he ordered them.

 Titch-Ella, though frightened by Vargas, was stubborn herself, and she stood her ground and said,
"Sorry, Mr. Vargas, but we are staying with the McCarthy family a bit longer as we still have much to teach them."
"What?" He shouted.

Again, he began trembling with anger. "How can you help humans? They never listen. You will be wasting your time."

Then he turned to Hoaby. "Are you willing to stay and waste your time, too?"

"Yes," Hoaby replied, supporting his friend, "Yes, sir. "I will stay and waste our life, I mean my life, Sir."

He stumbled through his words; he felt so small when the bullying bat was speaking at him in this way.

"Come on, son. We are wasting our time here."

Vargas dropped off the beam and flew past, nudging Titch-Ella as they passed, showing his dissatisfaction with her. Then they were gone.

"Wow," Hobby said. "They sure are angry. I hope you know what you were doing."

"Hmm, let us go back downstairs," she said, blocking out the bats' anger from her mind as they went back to see the nearly completed Christmas tree.

On entering the front room, they could see Adam lifting Clive to allow him to place the foil star on top of the tree.

"What does the star mean, Mum?" Titch-Ella asked.

"The star is something that we all try to follow in our life, for it stands for the brightest and greatest of all magic in our world – Love."

She smiled at the little ones when she heard Titch-Ella calling her Mum. She sensed that the Lepralites were giving back some of the love that she had shared.

As Katie turned on the Christmas tree lights, Titch-Ella whispered in Hoaby's ear, "Maybe we should stay a bit longer as these humans may have something they can teach us too."

The fairy lights twinkled and Hoaby thought one of the starry lights was winking at him allowing everyone to have a good laugh in the shadows of Mum's green heaven.

Adam sat on the couch with Clive on his lap and Cody next to him with two little Lepralites hugged against his other leg.

Mum and Katie shared the cosy single seater with Mum doing her usual twiddling of her daughter's curls.

There was no need for the TV this evening, for as the darkness fell, the curtains were left open for the lights to shine out from their home like a beacon on the hilltop.

Yes, for this evening it was a beacon of happy contentment.

****

5. Ma

Fifteen hundred euros. For a cat! Are you Nuts?"

Ma had just wanted to scream at her daughter for her lack of value regarding money. For fifteen hundred euros you could buy a lot of things. After she is married, the girl's house will need money. If they were frugal, fifteen hundred euros could go a long way to feed most families for two months. Even Johnny's funeral in its entirety only cost three times that. But paying that sort of money for a cat was beyond Ma`s comprehension. Ma had been raised on a farm, where cats were ten a penny. They were just one more necessity that had kept their sheds free from rodents and anything else that might be eating the food meant for the cattle, hens or horses, and the other working animals. There always seemed to be plenty of cats on most farms as there were usually plenty of small rodents to feed on; the farmers were happy to have them around for that purpose. There was no need to worry about them as they were always independent. If kind enough the farmer would often put some unpasteurized milk in a bucket for kittens to enjoy so they would feel at home.

So, it was understandable that Ma was shocked to discover that her daughter was, in her mind, silly enough to waste fifteen hundred euros on a cat. It did not matter to her that it was called a SIAMESE cat nor that they were seemingly as rare as hen's teeth. Whether it was Siamese, Japanese, or even French, that was a lot of money to waste. Ma knew she could not show her ungratefulness towards her daughter's gift as it was bought for all the right reasons. One being was to keep her mother company after her dad passed away, especially with the house going to be empty soon, or so Ma hoped. That was, if they could ever agree on a date for them to get married as Johnny, her dad's illness, had given her fiancée a great reason to delay their wedding. Or maybe it was a joint decision to wait as they were saving for a house, but whatever the reason, it was not being discussed with Ma.

Ma did like her daughter being around. She was always light and airy and full of enthusiasm for life. If not for her girl being around when the father of the house departed, Ma would not have known how to function independently after losing such a massive part of her life to the Heavens. Despite having four other children, they were all grown up, married, and spread out all over the country, living their lives and looking after their own families. They could not be there for their mother the way her youngest daughter was, especially with Ma having little skills in using laptops or modern phones to navigate through the modern-day online systems. These seem to have taken over her old world, which used to be one of ringing up or dropping in for a chat to do a bit of business. Clicks and enter replaced a lot of the shaking hands to do her deals. Her old world was running away, leaving her, like many others, scared of technology. Thank God for her daughter.

After the dust had settled from Johnny's departure, her daughter arrived home one evening with a cardboard box. It differed from the sort of box one would get in the post. This one had proper ventilated holes and plastic inserts. The box packaging may have accounted for some of the fifteen-hundred-euro cost. As Ma opened it, she saw the tiniest, cutest little kitten she had ever seen, despite its sharpened-featured face and abnormally skinny legs. Ma immediately envisaged her husband sitting in the box, for he, too, had pointed features. He had skinny legs and a large, pointy nose. When they were younger, she loved teasing him about that, and his scrawny chicken-like legs. But she loved every part of him. He could be described as a wiry man, but he was super strong for his size and a hard worker, especially with a shovel. His work colleagues had nicknamed him "Digger." And it stuck with him for the rest of his life, being well known in the neighborhood as "Digger. So, there was only one name that her new kitten would be called.

DIGGER.

Ma lavished her lonely love on the little cutie, which soon grew into a cat, and even though Ma did love having it around the house, as it kept her company in her lonely moments, sometimes it did annoy her when it brought what might be called its prizes to the front room. Nobody likes seeing a dead rodent on their good carpets. But she could not give out to him too much as he was just a cat. However, Ma did get very upset if she found her Digger eating these rodents; killing them was forgivable, even welcomed at times, but the thought of her angel cat devouring those vile things upset her deeply, and she would not hug her cat for ages over her distaste of where its mouth was.

All the truths of her cat's origins came to her at Johnny's remembrance service on the first anniversary of his passing, as she had met one of her daughters' old classmates who inquired about the new cat.

"Yes! We went to the North of Ireland to get him for you."

Ma was in disbelief that her daughter had gone far out of her way for a cat when so many were running wild locally.

"Oh, yes." The classmate continued." They are such a rare breed of animal."

Ma nodded, thinking it looked a bit different from the other cats.

" So, I suppose fifteen hundred euros was very cheap for a Siamese."

Ma spat out her tea in shock.

"Fifteen hundred euros, what?" She gasped.

"Fifteen hundred euros, of course," the girl replied. "My friend paid eighteen hundred for hers, but that was with full papers."

It was a long way from cat papers that Ma was raised. She had little interest in any papers. Her head was swirling. Making that sort of money would take a lot of baking of her cakes. Her daughter did work hard for her money driving up to the city every day, but the thought of so much money being spent on her cat…. Well, it was all too much for her.

For over a year now, she had not told her girl that she knew how much was paid for Digger. However, when Ma worried about money, she felt like renaming her cat Fifteen Hundred Euros!

But the romantic in her loves the name of her cat. As we all know, cats like to explore and know what is happening in their surroundings. They do not call cats "nosey" for nothing. When it goes missing as it frequently does, Ma's voice could be heard calling out "Diggerrr Diggerrr" all over the parish. The neighbors teased her, saying it was like listening to a call to prayer. "Diggerrr Diggerrr" rang out through the skies. It's a pity she was not shouting "Free cakes." they would say in jest, as her baking exploits were known to everyone. She had won many awards in cake shows over the years, even though she never entered them to win a certificate or a medal. She just wanted new people to taste her cakes and let her know that she still had retained her gift of producing tastes of delight, which her Mum had trained her in when she was still only a child. Baking was Mas' happy place. Watching the expressions on people's faces as they tasted her cakes was the best gift she could have ever received for her effort. There was not a wedding, christening, birthday party, or even a funeral in 40 years that Ma had not supplied in the area, and this Christmas had been exceptionally busy for her, as she always found it hard to say "No" to people who wanted her tongue-twisting delights. But she limited the orders now to her immediate townland.

Ma did not like driving or travelling too far. She believed her gift should be kept for the locals and those she cared for most. She always said that spreading love too thinly turns into mist that floats away on the clouds. In the past, yes, she had travelled to shows. But it was always with Johnny, her husband, who drove her, and he was the one helping her to set up her stalls. But now that her partner was no longer there, she stayed where she knew her surroundings well. However, with new neighbors in the area, she needed to showcase her delights for them. Being a woman who always built her world carefully despite her enthusiasm for wanting a stranger's smile after engulfing her cakes, she needed to know more about the new people who had moved into her world. They say animals reflect their owners, which may be why Digger always had to know what was happening in his area. For some time, she had seen her new neighbours around the village. She knew straight away that they were city folk. Maybe it was the fact that the lady of the house had taken the time to put on her makeup before going to the local supermarket, and their children had been combed and scrubbed before they were left loose in town. The locals usually went to the shop, keeping it as a quick pop-in, meet-and-greet exercise, and would rarely take the time to dress up unless it was a special occasion, gathering, or even going to the city. Ma's thoughts about others dressing up when there was no need to, in her eyes, showed a bit of insecurity about them, if they needed to look good, when picking up some spuds or chops from the local shop. Sur, the village shopkeeper, never wore a suit unless it was a funeral or wedding.

"Yeah, these newbies were most definitely city-styled,' she thought.

From talking to the postmistress, she knew that the McCarthy family had bought the vacant cottage behind her place. Ma was hoping that her daughter would buy that house. Being so close to her would have been nice, but her daughter dispelled that idea, saying that "there was far too much work to be done to it. Besides, it did not have all the modern solar panels and geo-thermals." Which Ma knew nothing of. But maybe it was that very reason that Ma judged to be so great, was the exact reason that her daughter felt the need to buy a house that was not close to her mother. Either way, the McCarthys are living in that house now as her new neighbour. She also found out that Mr. Adam McCarthy had managed to secure a job in their village Co-op store as a manager because of the evolution of the store, upgrading it from a farm shop to the modern era of the deluxe shopping experience, which was all a bit much for Ma, when her local farm shop is now selling washing machines and microwaves. Moving with the times was always difficult for her.

On thinking back, she remembered when Johnny started working there. He was moving vast amounts of lime and barley around in a huge old shed, which was now where the co-op shop stood proudly in the center of town, where before it was on the outskirts. Like all things, the past gets swallowed by the future. Ma's research also revealed that the child's health and breathing problems in the city brought the McCarthys to her village. Yes. Bit by bit, she was piecing together her puzzle of information to allow her to feel comfortable in offering her hand in friendship.

It was almost three weeks since the McCarthys had moved in behind her. The Christmas celebrations had passed, and the New Year cheering would be in two days. It is a moment of reflection for all, bringing loneliness to some. This time of year, Ma missed Johnny. She could remember them cosying up together in front of the open fire, with their tea and fancy biscuits that they might have received as a staff thank you from the co-op. She could remember the happy noises when her children were young after Santa passed by or going down with her husband to the big city to grab some sale offerings after the shops had reopened after their Christmas shutdown. Aw yes, those were the days when businesses did take a break. Not like the new normal of twenty-four-hour convenience.

"God help us oldies," she thought, "how did we survive without the modern-day shopping systems?"

She poured a cup of tea and sat at her kitchen table looking towards the back of her garden. It was hard for her to ignore her new neighbour's garden, overgrown with everything that was trying to climb over into her clean-cut area.

"Yes" she thought. "This could be the perfect time for an introductory chat."

She was sure that many people from her area would have picked up some Swiss roll cake or other sweeteners such a tin of biscuits from the local supermarket and came and knocked on the McCarthy's door welcoming them to their community with open arms. But that was not Mas' way. That was not how she was wired. Besides, between being busy baking, and the wet weather giving her a chill it had delayed her meeting with them. Now with all the McCarthys background known to her and having recovered from her chills she knew today was the day.

Today, for her, was a good day; the clouds were not laden with rain, and the air smelled fresh, and yes, again, the crows were making too much noise sitting in their usual lined out pompous manner on the electrical cable squawking down at the world. But that was all part of living in this area. Or was it? She thought as she pulled out the cake mixer from the cupboard. There sure are a lot of them! Was I so preoccupied over the last few weeks that I did not notice them? Surely it can't be. She started remembering her childhood. When her Mum departed life too early, leaving her desperately lonely while at the same time trying to run the family home. She was so young and carrying so much responsibility, which had been landed on young Margaret by her father's refusal to hire some house help. Her childhood was cut short; she had to cook and clean for both her father and brothers, who worked hard on the farm. It was a real Cinderella story with no Prince Charming around. However, there were crows! Many crows came, and with the crows came her two little saviors, Floreen and Doadi. Her little 4-inch angels had brought her love, companionship, and light to her darkest days. They had helped little Margaret through her years of struggle, even banishing the pain of losing her Mum. They had been, as her dad said, "her invisible friends," for he never met them. Her four-inch friends were there when she could no longer go to school as there was no time, with family and farm commitments coming first. And because of that, she had lost her classmate friendships. Goodness knows where she would have ended up if it had not been for them. Whenever Ma saw a murder of crows, it reminded her that she was not living alone. Back then, the loss of Floreen, followed by Doadi having to leave, had taken a chunk out of her heart that she could never fill. Johnnys' then-young presence had patched it up by giving her plenty of love. But it was not the same for her, even though he had always been there for her after her little friends left. He had even tried to help her with the chores of running that big, now-empty house before stealing Margaret away to marry her.

Surely not? she thought as she looked up at the busy crows on the overhead wires. Then, her thoughts reverted to the smell of burning gorse. Her best friend in the world did not return after trying to save the vulnerable animals in the undergrowth after the fire swept up the hillside, eating everything in its path. A tear trickled down her ageing cheek, but she wiped it away, reminding herself that some memories need to be carried in a deep pouch.

As the mixer turned the flour, the butter, and the sugar over with its secret delights, she watched the crows' behavior around the McCarthy's house. And despite their dog's noise, abnormally, they did not seem to stray far.

"I'm going to bake an exceptional cake because there could be a lot more than my new neighbours eating it."

 She smiled at her thoughts of the possibility that one day soon, she might have the chance to meet her old friend. Her pain was covered over by expectations, hoping against hope! Still, the mixer kept turning with the same rhythm as her thoughts as they spun around.

"Maybe that's unrealistic? Surely, he was gone by now.'

She questioned herself aloud as the mixer kept running. "How many years has it been?" she thought to herself. "Thirty-five or thirty-eight years? Where has the time gone?"

 Yes, every so often, she would think of Doadi and poor Floreen. But now it could be real again. The more she thought of the possibilities, the quicker she wanted the mixer to turn and the oven to bake.

"Why did I not see this before? So many crows."

Her mind began to race with anticipation of what the afternoon might hold. She took a quick trip upstairs to look out of her back bedroom window to allow her to see past the old apple trees into the back of the McCarthy's house. It looks like they were there. The curtains are open. And she could hear a young boy shouting at something. How big he was. Yes, they are there. I wonder, do they like chocolate cake? Then, a horrific thought popped into her mind. What if they are vegetarians or vegans? A lot of city folk have that complaint, she thought. She tried to remember what the lady of the house had bought when she had seen her a few days earlier. Oh yes, she bought chops. Vegans don't like chops. That should be OK. They should eat cake. And yes, they have children, and all children like chocolate. Yes, they should eat my chocolate cake.

DING!

The oven sounded off, and the cake was ready. She already had the icing prepared, but now Ma had to sit and suffer the time passing slowly while the cake cooled. It took two cups of tea to do so, tapping her fingers impatiently on the table, almost wanting to blow on it to cool. Still lukewarm, she smeared the chocolate coating over and around the cake. Then she wrote with her icing bag. "Welcome Neighbour."

Ready to close the house, she noticed her cat was again on the missing list. She slid open the patio door and called,

"Diggerrr Diggerrr."

But she was too impatient to wait for her elusive animal to return. She closed the door. With the cake wrapped carefully, she placed it on the passenger seat, then drove around the corner and pulled up outside McCarthy's house.

"They're here. I can see their car and somebody walking around inside."

She picked up her cake, checked how she looked in the car rearview mirror, and walked towards a new friendship.

****

6. A Sweet Encounter

If there was ever a time that the Irish humans would want to hibernate, it was the days after indulging in their Christmas dinner. It is the time of saggy, low-hanging bellies and stodgy minds, all caused by greedy eyes and willing tummies.

It was a blessing that both sets of grandparents avoided the McCarthy household this year, allowing them time to put their new home in order. But for Mum it was more about keeping the little ones out of everybody's sight. She loved Adams Mum but her one failing was her inability to keep any secrets. Like the time when Adam told her that he was going to ask Jane to marry him and he was saving up for a ring, but before the week's end, the news had got back to Jane. She had plenty of time to rehearse her surprise, as it was a further two weeks before he plucked up the courage to ask her. So, it was a good thing that the grandparents were heading to other places this festive time of year.

This Christmas dinner did include some of Mum's delights, which she would never buy for herself, as the rest of the family were unwilling to taste the Christmas fresh Brussels sprouts or fresh asparagus, which she loved to eat. As their two children followed their dad's eating traditions of meat and spuds, trying to keep their vegetable servings to a minimum as they believed it was wasting plate space. But now she had found two little allies in the family who fell in love with Mums' favourite greens.

It was during this food hibernation period, when most were waiting for the new year to begin, a stranger's car pulled up outside the McCarthy's house.

The morning of playing with new toys and noise had ended, with Mum taking time to potter before the lunchtime duties began. Adam had gone for a walk trying to burn off some of his Christmas extra storage off his waistline, which had caused him to have moved out his belt buckle one notch. He had taken Clive and Cody with him, in order that they try to diminish some of their energy levels, as both were far too busy disrupting what should have been a relaxing family day. Mum had just finished covering a piece of brown bread in strawberry jam for the little ones. They were running about on the kitchen counter and jumping up on the storage shelves to see what other jams the McCarthys had hidden, that they might taste. Mum was looking forward to sitting down for a few minutes as Katie was still upstairs in her bedroom discovering the many apps and uses that her new notebook laptop came with, which she had found under the Christmas tree a few days earlier and since, was engrossed in it, trying to ignore any of her Mum's list of jobs that were waiting for her to do.

Tap Tap Tap

"Who is that?" she wondered, as they were not expecting visitors, now that all the Christmas stop-offs and hi-byes had finished for another year. It was strange that Cody was not bounding down the hallway, barking at the front door.

Tap Tap Tap again.

Forgetting she still had her apron wrapped around her waist, Mum pulled the door open. A middle-aged lady stood holding what looked like a round present. She looked a bit odd to Mum, as she was not wearing any coat on this winter's day. Instead, only a pink cardigan buttoned close to her neck, and a pair of brown framed spectacles hanging off her beaded chain took pride of place at the center of her fashion sense.

"Sorry for calling unannounced, dear. My name is Margaret, Margaret Murphy from behind you. I live just back there."

As she pointed around the side of the cottage.

"OH, Hello," Mum responded as the lady began to edge her way into the hallway, continuing with her old-style country pleasantries,

" Weather has been awful. I would have been here sooner if

the weather had behaved better. Oh yes! I nearly forgot. I made you a cake to welcome you to our little community here. Yes! It's a great place we have up here away from the town, near enough but far enough if you know what I mean."

The visitor left Mum wondering if she was going to draw breath at all. She was halfway up the hall and heading for the kitchen by now.

Oh No! The Lepralites. They are in the kitchen.

Mum was panicking silently, but Mrs. Murphy continued,

"Everybody - that is my friends, all call me Ma, Ma Murphy."

She put her wrapped present on the table.

" Do you mind if I sit down? My legs are not what they used to be."

Without Mum having time to think, not to mind offering a place to sit, the lady's bum planted on the chair next to the round table. Mum looked around, trying not to draw Ma's attention to the fact that she was concerned about something, but she could not see the little ones anywhere.

Back while Mum was busy trying to catch up with Ma's barrage of sentences, in the hallway one minute earlier, Titch-Ella and Hoaby were running for cover to hide from the stranger. They had hoped up onto the open shelves over their favourite bread counter and had hidden behind the large jam pots and tea caddies.

"What's your name, dear?" Ma asked, knowing well who she

was talking to.

"I'm sorry," Mum replied, "I'm Jane."

Ma began her inquest!

"I understand ye are up from the city. Sur, aren't you a lot better up here in the country? They were saying your young lad was having problems with the city air. I can't blame him for that. I try to avoid the place myself; my daughter is up and down for work. I don't know how she does it, but she seems to like it. Sur, why wouldn't she? She has a grand fancy little car for herself."

Mum was getting frustrated by now, finding it hard to get any foothold in Ma's conversation, who was reminding her of an overactive woodpecker rattling out her words. She tried waiting for a comma or a pause in the lady's sentences so she could say something, but there was little room to get in.

"I understand you have a little girl too?"

Finally, a pause,

"Yes, we have Katie; she is eleven."

"And your boy?"

"Yes, Clive. He is seven. "

Off Ma went again!

" Poor thing. I know well what hospitals are like. When Johnny was ailing with his cancer, we spent more time there than anyone would want to, and where did it get us? Nowhere – sur he is gone now, well over a year and a half. It was his lungs. They could not do much for him, and he suffered terribly."

"I'm so sorry, Mrs. Murphy." Mum felt awful for her, as she began to see that her rattling words were masking a lot of pain.

"They say it was caused by either the asbestos or the lime around him as he worked in the co-op sheds in the old days."

Ma stopped momentarily to reflect, then continued, "Sur, looking for things to blame is pointless. It is what it is, and he's gone. I hear your husband is starting a job managing the place soon?"

"Yes, he was lucky enough to be offered a job there that would suit him. Sorry for my manners," again she was checking for any sight of the Lepralites. "Would you like a cup of tea and biscuits, Mrs. Murphy?"

"That's Ma, love. And I would love a cuppa, but I'm not one for the biscuits at all, thanks. Johnny was the biscuit lover in our house, he loved the chocolate covered ones. He used to dunk them in his tea all the time. It was funny when it would break in half leaving it floating in the mug and sur then there be a big panic to dig it out with a teaspoon. But it always would break up. Aw, yes, they were the days." Mum listened again as the lady was reaching into her past trying to find her husband. After a few moments, Ma was back running the conversation again.

"However, we could open the cake and try some. I baked it in a bit of a hurry. I hope it came out all right."

Mum smiled at Ma's brazen, forthright country manner as she picked the wrapped cake from the table and brought it over to the bread-crumbed covered counter, only diverting to clip the kettle on. Ma continued talking about her family.

"Yes, my other four are all grown and gone. But the youngest, my daughter, is still in the house. She will be leaving soon if all goes well. They had to put back the wedding because of Johnny's passing. But I'm sure it won't be long, and she will be gone too."

Mum began to unwrap the cake carefully, allowing its aroma to drift around the kitchen.

It was all too much for Hoaby!

He was hiding behind the large coffee jar next to the half-full sugar bowl directly over the cake, so he was taking in the full force of the sweet cocoa-swarming smell, causing his senses to be overwhelmed, leaving him in a hypnotic chocolatey trance of delight. Letting his little nostrils lead him to push outwards near the shelf edge, allowing him to suck in more sweetness. As he did so, the rest of his body followed, and over the shelf ledge, he fell. Trying to grab on, he brought the sugar bowl down with him onto the counter.

CRASH!

Sugar and breadcrumbs flew everywhere, with a blue-haired Lepralite sitting on the cutting counter in the middle of a mess!

"Oh No!"

Shocked, Mum tried to hide him, for the whole family had agreed not to tell anyone about their new family members to protect them from unscrupulous people. And now, here she was, with what she thought was the town's busybody putting her spectacles up onto her nosey nose and coming up behind her for a closer look.

OMG, what can I do now? Mum's thoughts just stopped, like a frozen second of fear.

"OH, my lord," Ma gasped, "are you okay, little one?"

Mum was surprised by Ma's response, for she showed concern for the little guy's safety and spoke as if she were talking to a child instead of some alien life form, wondering who or what these strange creatures were, "are you okay, little one?"

Ma looked across her split glasses at Mum and asked,

"Where is the other one? They always travel in twos, you know, where is she?"

Titch-Ella stepped out from behind the tin of flour on the middle shelf, showing her entire beautiful self to Ma.

"Oh, my word. You are a wonder for old eyes, so young and gorgeous."

Then, looking at the counter, "And you, I think you're a bit of a scallywag the way Doadi used to be."

Ma was in heaven. Even though she had suspected that Lepralites were in the area because of how the crows behaved, seeing them back in her life after such a long time was fantastic. She spent several moments reflecting on her past times. Then she removed her glasses, wiped her eyes with a paper hanky, and cleared her running nose. Mum saw that she had a past with these creatures by how Ma acted and asked, "Do you know our little friends?"

Straightening herself, Ma replied, "Yes, well, not these, but my little friends Floreen and Doadi were my closest friends in the whole world when I was a child."

Mum poured the tea, leaving Ma a few moments to acquaint herself with the Lepralites. They moved back to the table, holding side plates and their wedges of chocolate cake. Hoaby and Titch-Ella were sitting on the counter, taking in all Ma had to say. It was not hard to see that she had an exciting past, and they wanted to hear all about it; they were hanging on to every one of Mas words, not even being sidetracked by the chocolate aroma swirling around the room. Ma talked of when the little ones had come into her young life after her Mum's passing, about the feelings of being the only girl in a house full of rough boys and how the Lepralites had blessed her over the years. But then she talked of the day that Floreen went to Never Never Land after her father wanted to get rid of the gorse on the land and had set fire to it without telling her. And how Doadi and Floreen rushed towards the smoke when they heard the young animals cry out for help as flames ran up the hill, burning everything in its path being pushed by the wind. She recalled Doadi coming back three days later still covered n black soot from the smoke and charred dust with his singed hair and ragged kilt burnt from the flames, for he had done all he could to reach his partner, but she was gone. And now, being left alone as a singleton Lepralite, he had to go. He would never have survived alone, for there was now no other to draw his energy from. She talked of the barrier and the lack of forgiveness towards her father. What made it worse is that she could not tell him what he had done, as he never knew they existed, nor could she tell her father how they had helped her during the young years of her life, So, ultimately, her father was being blamed for something he had no idea of. Ma would not say a word as she was afraid to show or tell any of her brothers or father as they would laugh or insult the little ones as they were not kind people. She often felt their little love in that big old farmhouse after their mother left. Ma looked up to see Titch-Ella and Hoaby, who were now sniffling, with tears running down their cheeks. "Don't take in so much, little ones; it was all so long ago." Then, thinking in expectation for a moment, she asked the little ones,

" I suppose you never heard of a little orange hairy guy called Doadi?"

The two little ones looked blankly at her and shrugged up their shoulders,

"We are sorry we never heard that name, but we can ask" Titch-Ella added,

Ma said, "Like I said a long time ago."

Mum was still sensing that her lack of forgiveness towards her father was still eating her up inside, but she knew there was little she could say to try and close a wound so old. For now, she wanted to learn more about the little ones.

"Is there more of them around, with other humans, I mean?"

"Yes, I'm sure there are," Ma said, "but people do not talk of them, for they will vanish if they do. As the ancients did,"

"Ancients, who are they?"

"They are the Leprechauns, dear."

"But I thought they were only myths or fables, just like the Goblins and Fairies?"

"Ah yes," Ma responded, "we live in a clever world of little faith. One lacking in understanding of things that they cannot see. And if it means having to find faith, most people will choose to believe that it does not exist. But as you can see over on the counter, that world Is alive and well. And may I say, it is only the deserving people who get to spend time with these wonderful creatures, so you and your family must be as blessed as I once was. But if you ever try to explain your blessings to somebody of less faith, you might find yourself answering questions to a psychologist."

"There have been stories down through the years. One that sticks in my mind is about an American who came to Ireland and met an ancient. He decided to show off his Leprechaun and make some money. Even after the little guy had saved his life, this man contacted the movie studios to sell the story. Greed it's a terrible thing. Anyway, this was back in the 1950s. Not only did the little Leprechaun vanish, leaving the man looking like a fool to the rest of the world, but the greedy man died shortly after in some freak accident."

Mum was back again, trying to keep up with Ma's words, but she was left wondering about the value of truth in them. She went over to the counter and cut some small cake cubes for the little ones, leaving them to enjoy, and went back to Mas's stories, if for no other reason but to listen to an imaginative storyteller.

On sitting down, Mum asked again, "Where do these Lepralites come from? Are they from Leprechauns or fairies?"

"Sush will you," Ma responded, "Lord above. Don't ever associate them with fairies. They will get very insulted!"

Mum was a bit bemused by that statement, "why so…?" she asked.

"I suppose you heard of Fairy Forts."

"No, Mum replied. "What are they?

Ma had to remind herself that the McCarthys were from the city, but she still found it hard to believe that Mum had never heard of Fairy Forts. So, she went on to explain how they were circular-shaped earthen forts that could be found on lands across Europe. "These places, where no farmer would disturb. And the few that did, now have all sorts of bad luck dropped on them."

Then Ma stopped, reaching across the table, and taking Mum's hand, she slowed her spoken word to say,

"These little Lepralites that you have here, they have no badness, no hatred or anger and certainly no thoughts of wars. They think we should all live in a content world with only a willingness to help each other. If one does, for whatever reason, choose to curse or hurt them in any way, the little ones will vanish, taking back with them their love, kindness, and blessings. So, it's no wonder they do not want to be associated with the fairies, their kingdoms, or the revenge things that most of us have heard about."

Mum was a bit take back by Ma's stories of fairies bringing bad luck, for when she was a child and even with today the Christmas trees lights being called fairy lights, it was hard for her to imagine the beautiful little creatures in a waring state killing and cursing their enemies. But strange things became fiction before. But for now, she would put it to the back of her mind in the stacked fille marked to be proven! Then discarded any thoughts of such like and got back to try ng to follow Ma's words. But the part about the little Lepralites was she did believe the warning that Ma had given her, so she was trying to decide if Ma was just strange or a tall tale teller or if there was something more. Mum watched her getting up from the table. She looked quite normal as she went over and rubbed Titch-Ella's cheek with her forefinger, saying, "She would see them again soon," and moved away towards the front door. Then she stopped and shook Mum's hand.

" I think we can be good friends. If you are their friend, you most certainly can be mine." Then she unlatched the door,

" I had better get back, but if there is anything you think I can help with, give me a holler over the wall."

She hopped into her old car and drove away.

Mum returned to the kitchen to find an empty plate and two swollen Lepralites lying on the counter.

"What did you make of that?" she asked.

"The cake is delicious!" Hoaby muttered.

"No! I mean Ma's words?"

Titch-Ella interrupted," We try not to think of such things. We leave that big stuff to the Elders. I for one, have never met a fairy. I wonder are they real or maybe some google fiction." Then she smiled at Mum. It was a moment before Mum realised that Titch-Ella was just teasing her," oh you are so cheeky young lady."

As Mum cleaned the counter, she was not thinking of fairies or other mystic creatures that could be the cause of blessings or curses. She was just grateful to have Titch-Ella and Hoaby, and a lady who lived close by, who cooks fantastic chocolate cake and tells great stories.

****

7. High Moon

Sometimes, when answering some of life's questions, the answer is nearly always is I don't know why! It is just that way. Such as.

Why are Lepralites less than four inches tall when fully grown?

or

Why does everyone in the family call Dad Adam?

It never set out to be that way. Maybe when the children were toddlers, they heard their Mum call their father Adam? I don't think it had anything to do with him being much older than their Mum. Nor was it that his family suffered from a lack of love or respect for him, as he was always the calm in mother-daughter storms of disagreement. Or when Mum gave Clive a rough time over the state of his room, Adam was the one who would sit on the floor saying to his son," Come on, we will clear up your toys together."

No, it was just one of those things where Mum was called Mum and Dad was called Adam, and such was life in the McCarthy household.

Would you believe that the Lepralites followed suit - calling Adam just Adam and Jane being called Mum.

****

In the short space of time since the little creatures moved in, they had gotten very close to Mum and Adam, feeling relatively safe in Jane's mothering of them, as she was treating them just like two more of her children. Neither their small size nor different looks made any difference to her. They were given a lot more freedom than Clive or Katie when it came to them popping out whenever they needed to. There was no problem, once they let Mum know they were going out. The Lepralites seemed to enjoy the whole parenting lifestyle, which allowed them both to feel safe and happy. But it was all so new for them and certainly was not expected, as the only parenting they had ever received growing up was through their transference conditioning process that they had gone through, with different Elders who had worked their energy transference through their ebony-cut-styled walking sticks when they were still only baby Lepras. A clan's birth process would only happen every four years, with a maximum of eighteen sacks brought to life, for the energy they drew from the Elders took a long time to recover.

Titch-Ella and Hoaby's earliest childhood memories were of crawling around in an earthen hole in the ground surrounded by sixteen other Lepras just like them, with little room to stretch. Most of their time in the hollowed tight space, they spent wrapped around others on top of dry vegetation with the doorway to the burrows closed with sticks and fluff. Yes, it was a safe environment in which the little things grew their wings once they had pulled themselves out of their connected sausage-like sacks. This gave them plenty of connection to the other baby Lepras. They named it the" Daisy Chain Conductor Evolution" as these different creatures were fed before birth by a transference of energy that carried a joint pot of knowledge collected throughout the ages and passed across the clans. By joining with their kind, power would flow, revitalising each other. However, unfortunately, they grew up without parents nor hugs or touch from some natural traditional parenting Lepralites, so for Titch-Ella and Hoaby to talk, smile, and laugh with a human who treated them like their own children filled an empty void in their lives. One that they never knew existed until they started experiencing the human family environment.

Now.

At this point, we must discuss the elephant in the room, or should we say the bats in the room!

****

Bats, a group of bird-like mammals had entered the Lepralite community. Somewhere in their history, the little ones felt the need to be parented or protected and reached out to the bats; it could have been a case of opposites attracting. Who knows? Or was it pure gullibility on the Lepralites part, in thinking that every creature is just as good and kind as themselves?

But I think that in their innocence, our little friends asked for a favour from the bats and have felt indebted to them ever since.

The bats had a considerable hold over them, as they have been around forever, behaving like some protective detail or overbearing parents. This sometimes gets too much for the Lepralites who live by their code of freedom. Every so often, the bats have their uses, especially during the dark hours when they fly sorties watching for predators overhead of the travelling Lepralites. Their ability to foresee dangers whether it is predators or other dangerous situations such as human car traffic or changing weather patterns, which as we saw, can catch out our little ones quite easily. But the real dark side to the bats is their need to feel more important than others. When there is a favour given, everybody will hear about it, with the bats telling all who will listen just how great they were and why. Their self-sacrifice will always be well broadcast whenever they did the little ones a favour or any other animal for that matter.

If we are talking about animals that surround our little friends, we need to talk about the" day guiders." They would be the ever-present ones in the sky when the Lepralites are out and about during the daytime. These very clever, strong, black, loyal, robust, and speedy birds have an exceptionally long history with the little ones protecting and guiding them away from danger if needed. If there would ever to be a parent to the Lepralite clans, it would be the Crows. Some stories told of crows having given up their lives fighting off hawks and other predators, allowing their little friends time to escape the danger.

The need to get together on a regular basis was buried deep in the Lepralites' DNA. Without this, they would weaken, grow dull, then dry out to dust and vanish in the passing breeze. Socialising to rejuvenate was a priority. They choose the time of the full moon as their guide for many gatherings, with the month's moon cycle reminding them that they need to top up their energy. Or was it a case of following old human traditions? But either way, the nights of the high moon was a fixed date on every Lepralites calendar.

Tonight was the High Moon of the Rose.

Others call it the Brightness of Wolves.

It is the time in late January when the moon is at full circle, when the Lepralites meet. From early, the crows were squawking from the sky, giving plenty of notice of the night's festivities. For most Lepralites, it has been looked forward to for quite some time, like a human child would wait for Santa. I say most because, like humans, our little ones are not all the same.

Or, to coin a phrase," They come from the same cloth but have different colours."

A typical example of this is Snizzel.

Snizzel was born in the four-year cycle before Hoaby and Titch-Ella. They could remember him choosing to live away from the clan when they were very young Lepras. At that time, it caused a lot of talk, not only from the bats but also the other Lepralites, who found it hard to accept any Lepralite leaving the clan's sanctuary to go and live in a human environment. At the time, few had done so. It simply was not their way.

But as always, there is a story behind his need to go. The bats broadcast their version, which told of him being outcasted because of his ongoing illness and how he was spreading it out amongst the other clan members with his constant sneezing, which left him sickly with watery eyes and unhealthy looks. This, in their view, considered him a bad advertisement for a healthy clan. But despite him not looking like the poster boy of the Lepralite community, that talk was certainly not true. It went against everything that the Lepralite community believed in. Their love of sharing was always part of their makeup, but once again, the rumour tree was dumping out its lies. By taking something pure and turning it upside down, the rumour tree used its filth to weaken a beautiful community. It was clear the bats had spread that rumour rubbish. But like some humans, despite knowing its origins, many animals around the countryside needed to discuss it. In the newspaper industry, they would say that "it made for good reading." Despite the hurt that it caused, not only to Snizzel, but also to the reputations of the Elders and the rest of the Lepralite clans. But the truth always comes out sooner or later.

The truth was that Snizzel was born with a horrid allergy for any Lepralite to live with. It was Hay Fever.

Can you imagine what it was like for him at his birthing, coming out of those sausage sacks onto the dried vegetation that was there to keep all the baby Lepras warm? Instead, it just choked him up with dust.

Can you imagine what it was like for him when he lived in the forest and tried to play and travel with his friends in the fields full of pollen?

For two-thirds of any year, poor Snizzel has left on his own, sneezing, with his sizeable red water-filled eyes draining tears down onto his puffed hairy cheeks and dripping off his whiskers.

Or can you imagine the times he crashed while trying to cough and fly simultaneously?

The Elders were out of options as none of their regular potions worked on Snizzel. They knew of a kind, gentle man called Lord Dunken, who they asked if he could help treat the little Lepra, as he had a natural gift of healing all animals. Because of their love and care for the boy, they pushed all the Lepralite traditions and boundaries and asked for a human to help the young Lepra. It was all a sorry situation that such an occasion needed to occur. But Lord Dunken had many old remedies. One which eased his breathing and another to slow down his dehydration from his constant loosing of water from his eyes, for this constant loss of fluids was leaving him stiff, sore, and very dull in colouring. If this water loss continued from his little fragile body, then sooner or later there would come a time that Snizzel would not be able to find a water source when needed. And he would surely shrivel up and go to Never Never Land. After several months of treatment with a certain level of success, Snizzel decided to take Lord Dunken up on his offer to move into the main house, where he would be set up with a modern clean room with a ventilator that would clean the air of pollen, allowing Snizzel to breath more easily. Yes. Strange as it may all seem, it did save Lepra's life. However, it separated him from his clan, allowing that rumour to be born. So, when Snizzel was trying to deal with his homesickness, he also found himself trying to explain to the animals on Lord Dunken's farm why such a move was for the best and that the decision to move to the farm was all his. But again, like all rumours, some animals would always prefer them rather than listen to the truth. But things did settle, and ever since Snizzel was staying in the big farmhouse, he would venture out if the air quality allowed. Despite knowing how a night of a full moon celebration would sometimes damage his breathing, especially during pollen season in the summer months, he still had to go to rejuvenate with the rest of his clan. Life for him was a balancing act. He was always choosing the lesser of two evils because he would dull and disappear with the dust by not getting that connection. But being a Lepralite he was a natural born socialiser, and he did look forward to chatting with his kind. Now, he, too, was hearing the crows reminding him of the night's upcoming celebrations.

As the winter sun began to say good night, Hoaby got his kazoo ready, which he had found a few years earlier and had practiced ever since for these big occasions. He put it up on his shoulder and was now heading for the letter box flap on the front door calling out to Titch-Ella to hurry up to follow him. But he knew she could be a bit late as Katie had introduced her to mirrors, which she always had to check before going anywhere!

"Come on Titch-Ella. We are going to be late," sounded out through the house.

He struggled, pushing the kazoo through the flap, then he followed it outside dropping down onto the footpath. Many Lepralites called his kazoo a Wind Cryer as it sounded like a whistling hollow wind. Despite its cumbersome size, Hoaby always dragged it to the meetings to show it off to the others by playing louder than anyone else but not necessarily in tune.

It did not take Titch-Ella long to catch up to him, using her enthusiastic skipping walk while Hoaby was weighed down by his musical instrument struggling down the muddy pathway between the wet green fields and the old half-dead thorny ditches that were waiting for spring to revive them. Titch-Ella offered to help Hoaby with the kazoo, but he did not allow her to share the task, saying it was easier to carry it on his shoulder rather than take it between them. As they had to get it over the hedge row, two carrying it would be all too awkward, and flying certainly would not work because of its weight. But on they went, with the bats peeping and calling out from overhead as they darted over the travellers' pathways, showing them a safe passage to the large empty chestnut tree which awaited them on the upper end of the south-facing field.

By the time Titch-Ella and Hoaby climbed over the last bushy divide the distant lights along with the large round moon revealed to them just how dirty they had become from their travels. They could see the brightness of little lights floating around the massive tree that stood throwing its moonlit shadow down towards them. Their excitement began to overtake their striding little legs. Despite the weight they had with them, they could tell that they were running towards a beautiful evening.

The vibrations were growing stronger with each step they took until they were surrounded by what felt like a ball of energy buzzing around and through them. This lifted their light levels and cleaned their kilts. As they began to mingle amongst their own kind, all were full of colours from both their eyes and the scaled flight wings that hung sparkling from them. They weaved around the tree and the patched muddy ground on which it stood. Although its roots did seen to come from a drystone wall that joined into its tree trunk on either side which was covered in moss and bramble, the little Lepralites found it effortless to move over it.

It was going to be quite a special gathering as Titch-Ella noticed many new faces there, which sometimes happened when different clans travelled to mix their light sources and energy to amalgamate their power together as a group allowing them to become one with the gathering. All Lepralites shared the same nucleus in their make-up, which stopped any harmful or unclean energy grabbing their senses and spreading dark forces into their group or clan that would suck the good from them, leaving some groups carrying the blackened stained elements to the world. History has shown how easily this could happen even in the human world, causing unrest and wars.

Hoaby climbed the tree to join his fellow musicians who carried all sorts of instruments with them. After looking around, he smiled, knowing he was still the only one with a kazoo on the tree. He could see many different types of whistles and pompom drums and a ray of specially built harps and stick instruments and small spoons that were clattered together, making a rattling sound. Hoaby was in his happy place. It almost felt like a dream for him. Most musicians were now tuning up and practicing their instruments, which all sounded disorganised. It sounded terrible, like some sorry cat chorus that had come to town.

After a short period of chaos, the racket ended. The tree fell silent as the prayer Elder stood on the most significant outstanding branch and opened her wings, revealing a golden glow over the field below. Her power was overwhelming to all that surrounded her. Her glistening kilt reflected too many colours to count as they combined into a blaze of white light as intense as the strongest LED a human could make. Her little body saturated the surrounding area in a flow of love. She began to speak, not of a human tongue, but as a vibration. The musicians started to play gently, like a gentle breeze through the trees, as she spoke. The musician, bit by bit, slowly raising its volume then breaking up into their rhythm more and more, the momentum built. On doing so, the prayer Elder got brighter. Her vibrations could not be heard as the music drowned them out, but her colours moved around her body like a crystal ark spitting sheaves of light all around her. The music rose to fever pitch, drawing the local dogs to bark like wolves.

Then, suddenly, it all stopped.

Stillness fell across the land. The prayer Elders' colours dulled down, allowing her to mix back into the crowd on the tree. Some light chatter was heard, but before it could take hold, Olden, the Elder of the local clan, took his place on the outer branch. He raised his hands towards the heavens, showing off his ancient, coloured flight wings, and said,

" Tonight, we say to the Earth, sleep in peace and rest for soon you will awake in spring. We thank the clouds for giving us rain and the sun for its warmth. We thank the night for giving us cover."

As he finished his blessings, most of the Lepralites flew from the tree, gliding down onto the wet grassy field below. They linked their hands together, forming a vast circle to match the light shadow of the full moon overhead. Once again, the rhythmic music started, and the dancers' eyes grew bright as they moved to the right like a timepiece would run. They began to dance around and around in their circle, trouncing the grass to mud. Around and around, quicker, and quicker, the music started tap tapping, wood on wood, and crums popping to a frantic rhythm. Round and round they went. They then began to zig-zag in and out in their circular movements while still going around. If one did not know, we would think they had practiced their dance for days. But they had not, as it was just one more thing they were naturally born with and stuck in their makeup. Then, the music and dance slowed until the silence returned to the air. And the Lepralites flew back to the tree. They stood on the outer branches of it, looping hands again with one another, bringing their daisy chain effect into play. From the ground on the left to the bottom on the right, up and over the tree, like a monster canopy, a rainbow formed as their colours entwined with each other's, and it created a warm glow within each one of them. Again, it cleaned them from top to their toes. Then the Elder spoke the last word of the evening:

"Let us be one with the Earth. Let us honour the sun and be thankful for the joy that we can give. Let the ring of love burn eternal."

The field fell silent.

Once more, Snizzel was saying goodbye to his friends and clan alike. The winter evening was kind to his health with neither cutting cold nor pollen to choke him up. It had allowed him to delight in the clans' blessings and now he too was radiating health and colour as he skipped off into the night trying to whistle as he went. Titch-Ella used to feel sorry for the boy before, for having to live with a human. But not now. Since she and Hoaby had found out just how good some people were, her prejudgments of humans were diluted down to leaving her seeing more goodness in some people. She was sure that Lord Dunken was just as kind as the McCarthys, and she knew Snizzel was going back to a happy home. On thinking some more, as she watched the happy Chappy skip away, she began to dwell on the word home. More to the point her home. And the more she thought about her new home, the quicker she wanted to return there. The little ones all left down their own pathways from which they came, leaving only one big circle of mud behind them in the middle of the silent field. Each Lepralite now looked scrubbed clean and polished as though they had all just being taken out of a magical tumble-dryer. Their kilts glistened in the moonlight, and their eyes shone bright with joy driving away the winter shadows before them as they walked away from the now silent field. Even the bats, who controlled their sky's seemed in better form as the flight patterns resembled a prancing dancing flow instead of their usual darting movements.

With the extra pep in their step and the kazoo seeming lighter it did not take them long to push back the flap on the front door. Cody was happy to feel them, as Hoaby and his kazoo landed on top of him as he lay against the front door inside when Hoaby dropped from the letter box. Cody had tried to wait up for his two little pals to come home. But as usual, sleep overtook his enthusiasm. Surprised, he jumped from slumber, greeting his friends with excitement and slobbery kisses.

"Shush, Shush," Titch-Ella whispered in case he woke up the family. But he did not bark. He only followed them into the kitchen with his tail wagging. They were heading back to their favourite spot on the counter where the brown bread and jam pieces sat neatly on a plate, put there by their Mum, for she knew they would be hungry after the night's travels.

Yes indeed.

Once again, she had shown them that she was a caring Mum and that being part of a family was a good thing.

****

8. Soggy Owl

Being new to the area, Adam had no idea who his neighbors were. Nor did he know that the wild, overgrown farm entrance where they had found Titch-Ella and Hoaby belonged to a widowed farmer who had retired from working on his land and became a recluse.

Most people in the neighborhood did not socialize with him, as he was a person who had a lot more time for animals than his own kind. He had allowed much of his once-worked land to turn back into wilding fields with overgrown ditches. Even his sheds, which once housed cattle and hay barns, had become dilapidated, with creaking half-hinged doors and broken windows, allowing the weather to pass through them as they had become like open wind funnels. Its cobbled stone yard was overlaid with grass, and its gates had rusted, leaving only shadows of broken divisions. Many locals had stories of how he had given up living when he lost his wife, the love of his life, many years earlier. Others declared that the yard and the buildings had become haunted by her. But either way, most people kept their distance from him and his farm.

Meanwhile, Ireland's weather had returned to giving plenty of rain to North Cork as it hopped off the roof of the McCarthy's cottage. The two Lepralites settled down after playing time that gave them more time to get to know their new house. Already, they had found many interesting places to hide and seek between the hall cupboards and the long outdated disorganized kitchen with its old alcove eating area, the living room was by far the largest open area in the house, and they had studied every nook and cranny when looking out from their now-banished cage and since had flown over every inch of. It was also the warmest room, as the McCarthys kept heaping logs onto the stove. Even though it was cosy for the family, it was overwhelming for the Lepralites, who had to drink much of their water to keep themselves hydrated. They were not used to such dry air.

The most exciting place they had found in the house was behind the door under the stairs. It was a darkened chasm of old spider webs and dust. It was the only place in the house that Mum and Adam had not got to clean because of their lack of enthusiasm for facing such a spider fest. But for Titch-Ella, it was just one more adventure land where they could make up games of caves and hidden treasure, making tinfoil balls as coins and looking for things that had been hidden for years like old newspapers, burnt-out hairdryers along with an assortment of well-worn aged forks and spoons that some past house occupant had thrown in there and forgot about them. It was a place that in some ways showed the history of the cottage, for it was the one little room that its walls were not covered in plaster and its old timbers on its floor gave off a musty aged smell. One of the newspapers found was from the nineteen sixties. Even then most of the news was not too positive and was printed out on the now yellowing soft, thick paper, that still exuded that old familiar smell of days gone by.

As they settled in for the night, the little ones could hear the low whimpering screeching of an animal crying for help in the back garden. They found it strange that Cody was not at the back door barking, but he was exhausted from chasing Hoaby all day around the house. They both found a common interest in a game called hide and fetch. Where Hoaby flew and hid, little Clive would say "Go fetch," as though Hobby was the ball that was thrown, and Cody had to go and collect it. Thank goodness the game did not involve Cody picking up little Hoaby in his mouth, but it did mean him having to find Hoaby in one of his many hiding places by sniffing him out. But now the dog was sprawled across the end of Clive's bed, unable to wake. And for the little boy. He, too, would be in dreamland. Titch-Ella found it hard to believe that the two animals that had no time for each other when they first met, were now such good friends. She remembered how both of their first impressions of the other were so wrong as they butted heads for the first few days with neither of their strong personalities giving way to the other. Yet when she had the conversation with Cody it had revealed his hangups from his puppyhood which were not dissimilar to Hoaby's need to be heard. And as they settled into their all-equal family, it was nice to see them secure enough to allow their friendship to blossom.

The whimpering persisted with its shallow screeching. It annoyed Hoaby as he tossed on his bed,

"Will that silly thing ever be quiet? "I'm trying to sleep."

His daily exertions had worn him out too. However, Titch-Ella was far more tuned in and sympathetic to what was going on. She got off the shelf and slipped out to the kitchen, where she knew Mum was writing at the kitchen table with Katie by her side, for it was their girl time. Girl time allowed Mum and daughter to find joy in their common interests. Tonight, it was writing. They loved seeing words that were matching and then moving them around on a page. They pull them together into rhymes and sometimes poetry.

Titch-Ella flew in, landing on the tabletop amongst the disarray of coffee cups, books, pencils, and dictionaries. Katie quickly closed a folder cover as if hiding it from Titch-Ella, who had little interest, as she was on her own mission and was visibly impatient when she asked.

"Can you help me? There is a problem outside, and I cannot fix it alone, as the problem could eat me."

Mum and Katie were surprised and very curious by her request and why she would want to help with something that could eat her. It made little sense.

"Can you hear the screeching? Listen quietly for a moment."

Kate said, "Yes, I can hear it. It's not very loud, but I can hear it. What is it?"

"It's a barn owl," Titch-Ella announced.

"But I thought an owl goes towit, toowho?"

"No, not barn owls. They put on a screech, and I can hear his hiss and his screech. He is in trouble, and I know he will not last long with the cats around here."

Titch-Ella was showing her knowledge.

"Oh no," Mum jumped up from the table. "I will get a towel."

Digger, and the danger he carried, was the only cat on Mum's mind. Her fear for the health of the stricken bird was taking over, and she forgot about their writing projects.

"Where is it? Is it in the back? Come Katie. Get your coat and boots."

It didn't take long for the ladies to be dressed to meet the wintery night. Armed with a little torch and a towel, they opened the back door, following Titch-Ella's directions into the overgrown garden. They traced the dim torchlight to a side wall. Titch-Ella stood back on Katie's shoulders as she was the one holding the torch. Titch-Ella knew well just how dangerous these owls could be to small animals. The light found what looked like a drenched bird huddled under a bush trying to shelter. But there were few leaves to protect it from the downpouring rain. Even in the low light, on getting closer, it was plain to see how wet the animal was. Its light feathers were matted to its body, and a damaged wing was spread flat on the damp ground.

"Aw, you poor thing," Mum said. Taking the towel in both hands she leaned down to put it over the bird. Then she wrapped it up, being careful of the loose wing as she scooped it carefully off the muddy grass. It was in a poor state, showing no interest in fighting the human that had lifted it.

"Come on, let's go in," Mum said, knowing it was safe in her arms. They brought the damaged bird into the light of the kitchen, only hearing light hissing, showing the bird's displeasure.

"Can we make some room?" Mum nodded at the covered table, afraid to release an arm, ensuring the owl stayed wrapped in the towel. Katie quickly moved the books and pens to a chair, leaving a place for Mum to put the bird on the table so she could inspect it. She pulled the towel back from its head, wrapping its wings and legs in case it tried to get away. Its big, flat white face resembled a side plate with its helpless looking half penny-shaped brown eyes catching the love of Katie and her Mum.

"Go get your dad," she said. "We need the cage again. Don't worry, Titch-Ella, It's not for you guys."

Titch-Ella knew that as she began understanding Mum's sense of humor.

Adam came down the stairs in his pajamas. It was clear he had been called from his bed.

"What? What? What do we have here?"

"A barn owl," Titch-Ella explained.

"They are rare. Where did he come from?

"The back garden," Mum replied. "It seems to be the season for finding animals in trouble."

Adam smiled. "What can I do to help?"

"Can you erect the cage again in the front room near the stove, put an old blanket in the base, and keep it ruffled up if you know what I mean?"

Hoaby pretended he did not see Adam bring the cage back to the front room as he had no interest in moving from his shoebox despite Adams' cage pulling and clipping. But he did get a little worried when he saw the cage was being put back together.

"It's not for you," Adam said quickly.

But Hoaby stayed curious, watching Adam putting it back together and shoving a towel in, ruffling it at the bottom of the cage. Soon, the three girls brought in their new guest. Mum carefully reached into the cage, opened the towel, and left it hanging across the cream and light brown feathers. Its wing was still bent out of shape, so she carefully tucked it back in under the bird as it hissed. Hoaby's quiet fear suddenly turned into an explosive overdrive.

"Are you kidding me? They are savage. They will munch us into a thousand pieces. Why are you bringing an owl into the house? Are you mad?"

Mum looked up at Hoaby, who was now up on the curtain rail, as far away as possible from this predator.

"He is quite safe here. He won't hurt you. And he needs our help."

"Because we are all God's creatures," Adam added.

"Why here?" Hobby asked.

Hoaby seemed to have a short memory of how he and Titch-Ella had also been rescued.

"We all have a place on Mother Earth," Titch-Ella said.

"Yeah, I know, but it doesn't mean I like it," Hoaby responded sharply.

Hobby jumped back to his shoebox. He did not want to have anything to do with the owl. Titch-Ella and Katie watched as Mum carefully dried the birds' feathers with the towel. Then, they closed the clasp in the cage.

"Now Hobby. Look. He is locked in."

The bird's hissing turned to a high screech. And then a murmur.

"Now, girls, let's leave it to rest for a while." Adam said, "As I'm heading back to bed myself."

Kate wanted to stay watching the cage again. Titch-Ella thought it was a good idea, as Katie being around might help Hoaby relax. But still wanting nothing to do with the owl or Titch-Ella, he cheekily pulled the blanket over his head and hid from her.

"I think we need to take the owl to Lord Dunken," Titch-Ella suggested.

"Who is Lord Dunken?" Mum inquired.

"He is the farmer who owns the land where Adam found us."

"The old farmer below us here? I never knew we had a Lord living near us," Mum said.

"Well, he's not a Lord by human terms. But for his love and care of animals, he is known as "the Lord" within the animal community."

"Do you know him?" Mum asked.

"Yes, sort of," replied Titch-Ella. "I know some Elders who knew him."

By the morning, Hoaby was exhausted from being awake all night, afraid that the owl would attack him, dreaming that he had escaped from the cage. However, Titch-Ella slept just fine. During the night, concluding that Hoaby would not leave her rest, she had found herself somewhere else to sleep in the house away from her friends' fear, and was now fully rested and she was now wide awake with the rest of the family. Mum and Katie had got up early before Cody woke to remove the cage and its occupant and put them into the car boot. The owl was thoroughly dried out by now. Even though he was still very docile, Mum believed Titch-Ella knew best, and they should go down to Mr. Dunken's farm as soon as possible, even though Katie thought it should be the vets they should be heading for. But the decision was made. "Dickie Dunken" was the person that would give the best care. It was decided that Titch-Ella should stay home as Mum was still afraid of more humans meeting her little friend.

After the normal "where are my keys" and "I forgot this and

that" time from them, both Mum and Kate drove off down the road and turned left into the old overgrown driveway: high ditches covered with years of briary growth on both sides closed in on the passageway, creating a narrow-tunneled effect. As the car travelled slowly along the rugged road surface the old briars reached out, trying to scratch the car as it passed by towards the old farmhouse that was revealing itself at the end of passageway. As they pulled into the paddock area, the neglect began to worry Mum.

"Are we in the right place"? She asked.

"Well, this is where Titch-Ella said we should go," Katie replied enthusiastically, jumping out of the car.

"Be careful in case there are dogs," Mum said, unsure of the whole dismal feeling she was getting from the place.

"Come on, Mom, I can't hear any barking," Katie said, walking spritely towards the old front door.

Thud thud thud!

Katie knocked on the old, heavy-style door using its large brass knocker. But nothing. Again, she drew back the large brass knocker.

Again THUD!

"Maybe no one's home Mum?"

Then, the door started to be dragged open.

"What do you want?"

An elderly, roughly dressed man stood before her, clasping a wooden walking stick tightly like he was ready to hit somebody.

"Titch-Ella was right."

It was evident that he had little time for people.

Katie paused.

"Our friend said that you could help." She stuttered.

"What friend? I do not have friends. What do you want?"

"Well, we found an owl in our garden. I mean, we think he is hurt, and our friend said to take it to you."

The man's gruff, unwelcoming attitude changed instantly to a welcoming, caring face.

"An owl, you say?"

Yes, Sir. We have it in the car."

"Oh, let me see."

As he hobbled towards the car, "My old legs have seen better days" he said.

By now, Mum was opening the car booth, revealing the cage.

Immediately, he recognized the caged-stricken owl.

"Oh no, it is Donut. Where did you find him? He is one of mine."

The ladies explained the night's events, leaving out the Lepralites involvement. He reached into the now open cage, removed the towel, and carefully picked It out.

"Do you have more owls?" Katie asked with excitement.

"I'm sorry, Mr. Dunken, but she loves animals," Mum said.

"Oh, never apologies for loving animals, young lady. The world would be a much nicer place if animals ran it."

He paused and thought,

" Would you like to meet Cupcake?"

"Who's Cupcake?"

 "Cupcake is Donuts partner."

He saw Katie's eyes widen with excitement from his invitation.

Continuing the conversation, "Would you believe if it weren't for a group of children in the north of the country saving these beautiful owls? And telling everyone they were about to go into extinction, and nobody would miss them until they were gone. Well, what could I do? Of course, I had to give them some help. Until then, I had almost given up on humans until I heard their story. They restored my faith in people well, children, anyway. Maybe you guys can keep showing us oldies that there is a place for our wild animals on our lands".

They walked around the back of the house into the old, neglected farmyard. Holding the bird carefully, he asked Katie to open the large black door. He continued to educate his enthusiastic young student as they went,

" The problem with barn owls is when they get too wet, their feathers act like a sponge, and they become sodden until they become three to four times their average weight. Then, they cannot fly because of all that extra weight. Then, stuck on the ground, they are doomed to attack by ground active predators."

"I think that's what happened here."

"Donut and his wing?" Katie asked.

"Yes, that could be sprained like you would hurt your ankle" He explained.

In Dickie Dunken's arms, the owl was content, neither hissing nor shrieking, not even purring. Katie dragged back the large door, revealing a sizeable open timber and stone structure with straw on the floor. It was a peaceful place, with only the odd flapping wings of a pigeon could be heard. They walked over to the timber bench in the middle of the shed floor. He put the bird down and stroked the back of its little speckled-coloured feathered neck.

" Look," he said to the ladies. Then he rubbed his fingers, dragging back its feathers, revealing an array of shades from light brown to light grey. "Aren't, they are stunning looking birds?"

"Yes, you named him well, Mr. Dunken," Mum said as they approached. "He sure does look like a Donut."

"Yes, I name all our animals after cakes, even chocolate buns and anything else that is sweet that I know of. But this one will always remind me of Kitty's Donuts,

"Kitty?" Mum questioned.

"Yes, Kitty, my dear wife. God love her. She was as good at baking as she was with the animals. Her love of animals showed me that they needed our help. But now it is just me carrying on what she started."

"She sounds like an amazing woman," Mum said gently.

"Yes. She was. Every day I come out here, and when I walk in the fields and see the animals returning to the lands, I see just how right she was."

The ladies could easily see the love in Dickie Dunkens' heart for his departed wife, also for the wild animals that he shared his life with.

Without them noticing, another owl had glided down from the shed's high beams and landed on the table.

"Quietly," Mr. Dunken said, "Step back." Which they did. They watched the much greyer owl poke its little beak into Donuts' feathered shoulder and give a light purr.

Whispering, he said, "That is Cupcake. Look at the grey feathers on her back. That would tell us that it is female."

Donut began to respond to its mates' urgings, walking a bit and moving its wing slightly.

"See, there is nothing like the love of a good woman to heal a man's heart."

He smiled at the two reuniting owls.

"We had better leave them in peace."

They all walked out and closed the large door to let the birds settle back into their animal life without the presence of humans. As they stepped out into the yard, Dickie looked up, noticing a lot of crows gathering overhead.

"I wonder if there is a storm coming. Sometimes crows gather when the weather is about to change for the worse."

He looked skyward. "No, the sky looks normal."

Then he looked at Mum and asked inquisitively, using slow words.

"Who was your friend who said you should call here? My new friends have a secret. Do they?"

He looked searchingly at Katie, who was left feeling a bit uneasy in her guilt.

"What do you mean?" She asked.

Then, sure enough. There she was. She stood behind them on the edge of the once-used limestone water trough.

It was Titch-Ella. Without turning, he said slowly,

"Hello, little one,"

Within a blink, Titch-Ella landed back on Katie's shoulders.

"Hello, Princess," he said. "I wondered who could have brought these kind people to my door with Donut."

"I'm sorry, Mr. Dunken, but it's the only way I could get them to meet you and the owl needed…."

"Stop, little one. By their actions alone, they have shown me that I can trust them."

Then, turning back to Katie and Mum, he said,

"If it were not for our little friends here, I don't know what I would have done when my wife passed away. They kept love and kindness around me when my heart was tearing itself apart. They truly are a blessing."

"Yes, I know," Mum replied. "We are lucky to have them."

He turned back to Katie and asked,

"Would you like to return sometime and help this old man with the animals?"

Katie smiled with acceptance. "I would love that."

"Thank you so much. Drop-down when you are free, and don't be trying to ring me on those new fan dangle phones as I don't have one; they are a nuisance," he said. "We will see how Donut is improving over the next few days."

He then smiled,

" It's you children that are the future soldiers for these animals."

Mum was feeling angry at Titch-Ella for not staying home as she was supposed to. And for not trusting her enough to let her know that mister Dunken and the Lepralite community had what seemed like, a long history. She wanted to scold her the way she would have if it were Katie or Clive who disobeyed her and had not told her all the facts. But she did not, for she understood that Titch-Ella would always be a free spirit. She also appreciated that it probably was not her business what interaction they and Mr. Dunken had over the years. But it would have been nice to be told a bit more information which would have allowed her to trust the elderly man a bit more. Maybe it would have allowed her to be freer talking with him. But she was now happy with the fact that if the Lepralites trusted him, then she could feel at ease with her daughter spending time at his farm. Mum knew deep down Titch-Ella was a self-thinking little animal that would always have a part in her, that could not be controlled or trained in human manners. She would always be free; she knew that if the family did not accept that, they would lose the Lepralites.

By the time Mum had driven home, she had decided to love and accept them for who they were and not give out or try to change them in any way whatsoever.

****

9. Plan or No Plan

Give me a plan but then a change of circumstance, and I will give you back no plan. When people talk about three or even five-year plans, they also talk about what ifs?

With them talking of so many ifs, the so-called iron-clad plans are merely myths or fables that may or may not come true in their future.

****

Mum knew this. That is why she and Katie had drawn so many plans for their future deluxe country garden, as they could not tell what they had to work with. For now, the garden was a briary mess, looking far worse than any of Dickey Dunken's areas. They had often tried to look beyond the first row of overgrown hedges and bushes, but the only thing they could see deep in the garden were two apple trees near what looked like the back boundary wall and Ma's house upstairs windows some distance behind that.

But all this was about to change, as two of Ma's husband's old work colleagues were coming tomorrow morning. Mum decided to get to bed early as she wanted to be up in time to meet them, as Adam had started his new job a few weeks earlier, his normal reliance could not be counted on. She picked up the Irish mythology book, which she had treated herself to, and started to read about the Dance of the Leprechauns. Except Adam, the rest of the family were in their beds. Her heart was still on guard, fearful for the future of the Lepralites and their community, which she still knew so little of. That is why she had read so many old Irish tales of late, looking for any connection to her little ones. She was working on two assumptions: first, that there is never smoke without fire, meaning all mythology was founded on some truth, and, that the path from history will always lead to the future Some of Mas conversation about the darker sides of mythology did upset her. When she was a child, the fairy and goblin books were always stories that would transport her imagination to beautiful places and happy people, taking her away from her sometimes-hard city reality's.

For some strange reason she awoke in the middle of the night still with her book in hand, and a large crow was sitting on the end of her bed. Its dark oil slick looking feathers were layered as black as the moonless night, with its piercing, lit brown eyes calling out at her.

"What are you doing here? You do not belong here! This is not your house," the bird shouted.

Mum sat up sharply and grabbed her sleeping husband with one of her hands, shaking him frantically.

"Wake up, wake up, will you, for goodness's sake, wake up, Adam."

But he did not stir.

"What do you want?" she shouted back at the overbearing bird; she felt her heartbeat against her ribs as she prayed the crow would not attack them.

The crow let out an unmerciful squawk of warning.

" You are going to kill all the animals in the lovely garden. You and your machines will tear our world apart."

" Wake up, Adam, for lord's sake." Mum shook him again.

 "I am not going to allow you to do that!" Its squawk was thunderous, but it still did not wake Adam.

"Who do you outsiders think you are?" The bird moved across the timber bed end in a shuffling, disturbed motion, moving its wings, wanting them to flap, but they just tremored in anger as he kept roaring down at her.

" Have you not learned anything from our little ones you undeserving HUMANS?"

Mum could feel sweat running from her forehead as she

begged her husband to wake. A loud machine started trying to drown out the bird's anger.

"WHAT ARE YOU DOING? THE ANIMALS."

Its squawk reached a fever pitch, trying to fight the sound of the machines revving. Then up it jumped, opening its wings, and smashed its way through the bedroom window on its way out. The machine kept revving over and over. Then, something grabbed her. She turned away from the cool air left by the opened window to face her kind-faced husband.

" Love, you need to wake up. The gardeners are here." Then he asked, "Are you okay? You had a very restless night."

She felt a bit of her normality returning on hearing a machine being revved below in the garden.

"Tell them STOP; I will show them what I want done in a minute."

Adam smiled and lovingly kissed her cheek. She felt he reminded her that he would always be there for her.

"The children are in the car waiting to go. I will drop them off at school on my way to work. I'm sure the job will wait for a few minutes longer."

He straightened his tie and gave her one more smile before he left the room.

A few minutes later, she came down the stairs fully dressed, ready for the day ahead. But still, with her thoughts firmly wrapped in the nightmare she suffered, she tried to self-analyse the crows' shouted words.

Do I feel like an outsider here? I don't think so. Maybe, it was my inner fear of hurting animals during the garden restoration. She thought of a way to get her two little ones to check the undergrowth for any small animals that the gardener's machinery might harm. Then she had a thought and called out to Titch-Ella and Hoaby to wake up so she could ask them.

"When I am in having a chat and a cup of tea with the gardeners, will you guys do your thing and have a quick run about and let me know if there are some animals they need to avoid?"

Titch-Ella thought Mum's idea was one of caring and wholeheartedly agreed and was enthusiastic to help. However, Hoaby was still rubbing his sleepy eyes, trying to understand what his pal was agreeing to.

Mum went out to meet with the two roughly dressed gentlemen waiting in the garden, introducing herself first and thanking them for coming so quickly.

"Ah, you're welcome"" one of the men said, "sur anything for a new neighbour."

"Thank you; would you like a cuppa? I have a quick plan outline showing you what I have been thinking."

As they all walked in the cottage's back door, Mum saw the little ones disappear into the undergrowth, after coming around from the front door letterbox.

"I was going to say clear it all, but I changed my mind last night."

By now, the teapot and two wedges of chocolate cake were

on the table. The moment the younger of the two men left the cake to touch his tongue, he said,

"Aw! Ma's cake." Mum smiled; "Unmistakable," he continued as he slowly chewed through the chocolate spongey delights, paying little attention to Mum's plan as she explained it to the older man. "Ya, that woman is a blessing to us all who have a sweet tooth," he interrupted again. He was starting to annoy her. Mum was beginning to think that she should not have produced Mas cake until everybody understood what she wanted.

One essential part was missing to complete her garden. Her double bird box was a surprise she had planned, and she wanted it screwed to one of the walls or trees. She had designed it to put two up and join them with a plastic pipe, giving two rooms for her little ones to spend time outside, keeping them safe from Ma's cat or other animals that would wish to hurt them.

In the meantime, Titch-Ella and Hoaby were skipping, climbing, and rummaging through the shadows of draping canopies of dead leaves and high yellow grass and some dodgy-looking stray old briars that once carried an age of blackberries. As they neared the back fence in the left corner, they found some old logs stacked and covered with moss. The Lepralites could hear a slight movement coming from under the stackings. Slowly, they crept into a hollowed-out room with old, dried grass and small sticks on the ground.

"Oh, look, Hoaby, it's Prickles."

"Aw, Yes, it is," Hoaby replied," I was wondering where he

went to."

"Hibernation, Hoaby. Hedgehogs need to sleep during the winter." Titch-Ella reminded her pal. Feeling slightly insulted, Hoaby huffed, "Ok, what now are we going to do?"

The hedgehog twitched, balling himself tighter, showing the world he was not ready to wake up.

"We need to tell Mum," Titch-Ella said. Ushering him to continue looking; they moved across the back boundary fence, then back towards the house, they swept around two large trees and bushes back towards where they had found Donut and back out onto the footpath, where they skirted carefully around the side of the cottage making sure they would not be seen. They crawled back in through the letterbox flap. They could hear the gardeners starting up their large, noisy strimming tools as they called out for their Mum to tell her about Prickles the Hedgehog, who was sleeping under a pile of logs down the back of the garden.

"Great job, guys, thank you." Then Mum turned to go out to the gardeners to tell them to stay away from the back left corner of the garden until she returned from the shops.

The two gardeners started hacking, pulling, and dragging their way through the garden, leaving only the established bushes standing while pulling out the old dead vegetation, with everything taken out and loaded onto their truck as they cleared their way through the long garden. Mum could smell the thick, heavy waft of cut rotting grass that hung in the windless, dense, foggy air over their hill of houses. Her mind was full of thoughts as she hopped into her car to drive down towards the town. With the gardeners now working hard, she could see that it would be finished in little time if they kept up their pace at which they were working. She was content with all that was happening in the garden. However, last night's nightmare was sitting in the back of her mind like a puddle full of questions. What did it all mean? Or did it mean anything? Was it all caused by stress or caused by all the new changes over the last few months in her family's life that sometimes left her feeling out of control? It was many years since she had had such a horror-filled night.

But for now, it was all about the little surprise she had planned for the Lepralites as she steered her way down the narrow boreen, to connect with the main road on the outskirts of the town. Still cautious of her new surroundings, she headed towards the new farm shop where her husband worked. She was unsure how he would feel about her just walking in on him. Would it leave him feeling embarrassed as it was all new for him too? She thought maybe she should have told him that she was coming. I hope he doesn't mind too much. As she swung her car into the car park, turning off the ignition, she checked in her car mirror to ensure no garden debris had stuck to her. Then she walked into the large open expanse of retail space. She imagined the shop would be smaller from her time talking with Adam about his job, but it was bigger than she had pictured. Despite there being a lot of people in there, it did not feel crowded as she walked freely around looking for bird boxes while at the same time keeping a lookout for her husband. But she could not see him. She browsed along the full shelves stocked with many different brands and items until she came across the boxes she had imagined: about one-foot square and sixteen inches high with little pitched roofs. On looking for a matching one, she found one the same size but in a slightly different style,

"Ah, that will do," she thought. A young shop hand saw her beginning to struggle to get the second box into the shopping cart and offered his help,

" Hello, my name is Adam. May I help you?" She smiled. Maybe, all that work here are called Adam, she thought as the young lad loaded her trolley.

" Thank you, Mrs. McCarthy," he said when he finished.

She asked how he knew her name, a bit taken aback by him knowing her name.

"Oh, that's easy," he replied in good humour." Sur, didn't my dad and us bring you the Christmas tree? It's a small place around here. Can I get anything else for you?"

"Maybe some wire to tie them up with?" he added.

She could tell he was learning quickly from her husband as it was like listening to his miniature, looking for the shopper to spend a little bit extra while at the same time being helpful. "Yes, please, Adam, could I also get a four-inch plastic pipe joiner?"

"OK, I won't be long. I will meet you by the cashier till."

He walked away, then asked her, "Will I tell Mr. McCarthy that you are here?"

"Yes, please, Adam, if he is not too busy, that would be nice."

Mum pushed the trolley slowly towards the checkout area, taking in some other things the shop sold. It took a few minutes for the lad to return with a small roll of wire and a bit of round plastic pipe in his hand.

"I am sorry, Mrs. McCarthy, but Mr. McCarthy is down in the yard doing a stock take, as there is some big load due later."

Mum paid for her shopping, and the lad loaded them into the car for her.

It took her just fifteen minutes to pull up behind a lorry full of her garden waste. She carried the two bird boxes around the side of the house and hid them from the Lepralites. When she saw her garden, it looked like it had doubled in size. Looking like it was striped within an inch of its life, the gardeners had only left two big apple trees and three bushes along with what looked like a once-used goldfish pond, which now was full of old sticks and rubbish that must have come from the garden once upon a time.

It was now getting close to lunchtime, so Mum offered the working men more tea, who decided they would have it outside because they did not want to destroy the kitchen with their dirty boots. Mum carried out tea and sandwiches, and you guessed it – Yes, of course, Ma's cake! She was amazed at the transformation of the garden. She asked to mound some more earth near the old logs where Prickles slept and cut back more of the hedges, and the significant extra job was to clean out the old pond area, which the men readily agreed to once they saw the cake! Mum also asked them to hang the two birds' boxes at a high point on the larger of the two trees, joining them wall to wall with the plastic pipe, explaining her vision to them. They were a bit bemused by her elaborate birdhouse, but she just said, "I love my birds." The workers accepted what she wanted and ate their cake as it was not their house. She gave them everything she brought to the shop, saying they should be safe from the cats.

Then, right on cue,

"Diggerrr Diggerr." One of the men burst out laughing,

" Ah, Ma's call to prayer."

When the other said, "Ya, we better hang that birdhouse high, especially with that frigging killing machine living behind you.

"He sure is a weird-looking cat." the older man commented.

On bringing Clive and Katie back from school, Mum saw that their garden was back to how it should be, even though it still needed some time for the leaves to grow back on the hedge and a good fall of rain to clear the smell of torn vegetation. Looking at the apple trees, she saw her two bird boxes hanging neatly with the plastic pipe joining together.

" Adam will love this," she thought.

The younger of the two gardeners approached Katie carrying a wrapped towel. He bent down and laid it on the grass.

" Look, I have something to show you."

Katie watched in wonderment as he unwrapped the towel.

" We found this at the bottom of the old pond. How it is still alive? beats me, with all the dampness in there. Maybe, it was the apple that saved her?"

Opening the wet towel revealed a little female hedgehog wrapped around an apple. It was still sound asleep.

"Oh, you poor thing," thought Katie.

"You had better wrap it up and take it to the vet."

"No, I don't think so," she said as she rewrapped it. "I have a friend who will know exactly what to do."

She got up and ran into the front room, calling for Titch-Ella and Hoaby.

"Look, look what the man found." As the little ones flew towards her, she rolled out the towel on the couch.

" Wow, two in one garden," Titch-Ella said, "that's strange."

On looking at the spikey animal, Titch-Ella suggested that when the gardeners have left, they put her in with Prickles as he has a nest, and she needs warmth. "I don't think he will mind too much."

The gardeners didn't take long to put away their tools on the truck and drive off down the boreen. Mum stood at the gate waving goodbye and shouting thank you, grateful for the transformation their hard work had created. She could see a white car pulling over in the distance to allow the gardener's lorry to pass. Then, it began to move again up the hill towards her. As it got closer, she could see that it was a police car. Her mind returned to the angry crow the night before as she began to sense that bad news was coming towards her. She had not seen the garda up here since they moved in. Her curiosity and worry stopped her from returning to the cut garden, where she knew she would find her four children putting the newly found hedgehog into Prickle's nest. As the car drew closer, she began to worry. Maybe being raised in a big city brought her fear of what they might have to say, as police rarely gave good news when they knocked on the city doors. Or was it those lasting visions of the crow in her nightmare and Adam not waking up? The white-marked car drew closer bit by bit, second by second, meter by meter. She thought more about the dream where her husband did not hear her call for help and the sound of the smashing glass as the bird had left the bedroom. Mum could hear Clive shouting that he wanted to put the hedgehog in the hole and being told to "shush and be quiet" and that he would wake it. The car kept getting closer.

Mum's eyes looked down, not wanting to see what was coming, and followed the car wheels as it slowed and stopped in front of her. Keeping her eyes down, she still had no wish to look at its occupants for what news they might bring. The back door opened.

It was Adam.

By now, her brain was moving in many directions, as she did not know whether she should be hugging him or shouting.

" We were hoping you would be home, love. The chief here wanted to meet with us and discuss some potential security issues with shop keys and the spate of ransoms and robberies of late."

Maybe, this was the country way, but it just scared the wits out of Mum. She just smiled briefly at the Garda and gestured to them to come into the cottage. Adam continued.

" I said we might as well all chat up here, as there could be a bit of Ma's cake on offer.

As the Garda shook Mum's hand, welcoming her to the area, her only concern now was if any cake was left over after the gardeners feasting on it!

****

10. Finding Doadi

It looked like winter was finally left behind as the clear spring skies were starting to warm. Some bluebells and crocuses had found a ditch to show off their spring colours as Titch-Ella and Hoaby passed by on their quest to find Doadi or at least find out what had happened to him. The sad story Ma had told them left Titch-Ella finding it hard to dismiss the thoughts of the shadows of pain that still affected Ma so many years later. It bothered her how a Lepralite could be involved in leaving her with such sad memories. In Titch-Ella's mind, the whole story had to be investigated appropriately to help Ma clear those deep shadows which still follow her today. Those shadows were made by the pain of losing Floreen and the lack of forgiveness towards her father for lighting the fire. Titch-Ella had to find this Doadi character, for he held the key to allow Ma to heal.

She had no idea what clan he had come from.

Usually, these puzzles were easy to solve, but this all happened so many years ago; it had turned into a cold case. They needed to find and talk to Olden, one of the Elders. If there were anyone who could shed some light on this, it would be him. Even though it had all happened forty or so years ago, Olden had the age to remember those years, which could point them towards this Doadi fellow. Hoaby had put up many good arguments why Titch-Ella should leave this quest go," too long ago" being the foundation of the reasons given. Why are they wasting their time tracking down a Lepralite with such a strange name that will probably be in Never Never Land many years by now? The whole expedition was pure silliness as far as Hoaby was concerned. He also realised that he would lose a lot of playing time with Clive and Cody by going on the trip. All wasted because his pal wanted to try and solve an age-old mystery that she wasn't even asked to get involved with. Was she being a crazy young busybody? She probably was, but he knew he could not leave her to go alone.

By now, it was mid-morning, and Shefa had not eaten yet, though she was enjoying the welcoming sun's warmth on her back as she sat on top of some phone lines. The empty feeling in her belly reminded her that it was too early in the year to enjoy her usual abundance of field mice and unsuspecting little rabbits. Even the opportunity to steal a magpie or crow's food was scarce this year. Maybe they were getting wise to her tricks. Perhaps she needed to devise new ways to find food until her hunting grounds showed more signs of life again. Even though there was a great view from where she was, it was not a very fruitful surveillance point. But it was a good place to rest while at the same time keeping her wisdom about anything else higher up in the food chain, wanting to remove her. She flexed her talons and pulled back her wings, drafting the air under her, pulling her skyward back to her happy viewing place. She climbed higher, stretching her wings in a slow, striking movement. She knew how good she looked in the air with her cream and grey colours boasting to the sun as she glided at high altitude with her personified arrogance, letting her air sweep past from her beak to her fanned tail feathers. Then, turning around and facing the wind, she was lifted higher by her enormous wingspan, at least twice the length of her body. She surveyed the open fields with her sharp, telescopic eyes. By now, she was several hundred feet above McCarthy's rooftop and could see the tops of the maze of trees in the forest behind. The water that cut the wet, matted lands in half, glinted as it flowed towards the village. She could see the dull green and slate roofs of Dickey Dunken's dilapidated old farm looking up at her. She had often grabbed food from his disorganised lands, which were usually full of tiny creatures that regularly multiplied as they were not disturbed by active farm machinery. "Maybe that is why there were so many of them?" she thought, looking forward to them returning from their winter hiding. She kept glided, surveying the long fields below that led toward the outskirts of the town. Most were waiting for the cutting with the plough and harrow blades that would churn up the earth, yielding all sorts of delicious worms as the ground was opened again. "They will have to do if there is nothing more significant to munch on." Furthermore, she turned, banking, turning her beak to face back up the next hill to bring her back to the other end of the forest. Then, she stopped by changing the direction of her wings and holding her position after noticing a blue moving speck on the edge of a large, expansive grass-covered field. She thought she needed to drop a bit lower to see more.

" What is that?" she asked herself. Pushing her head down and tucking her legs and sharp claws in under herself, the hawk shaped back her wings and divebombed towards the little animals on the ground.

Even though Hoaby had plenty of exercise playing with the lads at home during the harsh winter, Titch-Ella was more likely to have spent much of her time with Katie doing teenage girl stuff, which was not so energetic. But it did allow for schooling in the art of makeup, along with looking through Mum's outdated fashion magazines, which they had discovered stacked on the floor in the corner of her bedroom that were waiting for a shelf. It did annoy Titch-Ella that she could not try on Mum's old clothes that they had found buried in the back of the wardrobe. Not only was she way too small, but also there was the issue that she had been born with her clothes. Unlike humans, they were attached to her body, so she could not take them off. So, to put new ones on, Mum suggested they could make some smaller clothes for her. But that would mean they would cover her flight wings, rendering them useless, and if it were a new top we were talking about, it would not sleeve around her arm wings. Another idea was to get some sticking tape and stick clothes on the front and another on her back. But that would not look one bit fashionable.

Today, she was grateful for not wearing fitted human-like clothes as she felt bloated, and she would probably burst out of them after indulging in far too many of Ma's cakes and Mum's brown bread and jam over the past winter weeks. So much so that she felt her rounded belly touching the grass stalks as she struggled to fly. After travelling across nearly three fields, her unfitness caused her to shout out to Hoaby that they needed to rest as her arms were hanging off her with tiredness. After a bit of quick-witted Hoaby teasing over her lack of fitness, they landed on the grass near the ditch to rest. Relaxing out on the warming ground showing her open wings to the heavens and sucking in the sunlight's energy, she began to think again about Ma and how strange it was that this Doadi guy never returned to her. Imagine if something happened to Hoaby - Would she go back?

" Of course, I would."

Then she thought, "Would Hoaby, though? Now that's a 50/50 question with his mood today. Maybe that guy Doadi is like Hoaby. Perhaps, he had also picked up a bit of attitude from Cody. That's funny," she giggled to herself.

"Now I am just going to relax for a few minutes and listen to the light wind in the trees."

At that time, Hoaby was sitting up fiddling in the grass, looking for clover, for he loved its sweet taste. But today, only tiny sprouts which tasted bitter as their leaves had not yet developed. Out of the corner of his eye, he noticed two crows flapping toward them. As they got closer, he saw how frantic they were moving. They rushed past just over his head, squawking.

" Get out, Get out,"

"What are they squawking about?" Titch-Ella asked in her relaxed, sleepy voice. Hoaby sensed something was not right and stood up to look around but could not see anything to his left or the right. Then he scanned across the field but could see nothing except grass. He then lifted his chin from his chest to look up. His curiosity turned to panic as he started roaring to Titch-Ella.

"RUN "

She opened her eyes.

OMG! Hopping up at high speed, she followed Hoaby into the ditch.

Was it too late as they ran through the briars, bushes, and undergrowth, for the bird was right behind her,

"Faster, Hoaby, faster, it's catching up."

She could feel the bird's sharp beak tapping off her head as she ran. Then, jumping over a branch slowed down the bird, but only briefly, as it had to go under it.

Hoaby shouted, "Follow me!" as he jumped into a hole and down the burrow. Titch-Ella was behind him as they crawled downwards until they entered an earthen room with fluff and dried grass. Titch-Ella's thoughts added to their immediate worry after realising where they were now. Was this a case out of the frying pan and into the flames?

"Oh no, Hoaby. I hope the Mummy Rabbit is not here," they had entered a baby's burrow, and if there were a doe, a female rabbit, she would start protecting her little ones with her dangerous temper.

But now they had more pressing matters, as they could hear

the bird clawing at the ground outside the entrance, and dried ground earth was rolling down on top of them. The bird then shoved its head into the hole, trying to follow them. But it was too big, so it shrieked down at them and pulled back out. It tried again, clawing the ground, then ruffled away, giving up. The terrified Lepralites sat for a few minutes, not saying anything before Hoaby, who was feeling a bit safer, said.

"Wow, that was too close," and they crawled out of the dark hiding place, thankful that they had found it in time and that it was empty.

Shefa felt disgusted with herself. She knew these little things should have been part of today's diet, but she lost them by a whisker. If only she could be back as fit and sharp as she was last summer,

"What were those things? I never got to try them." As she clambered back out of the undergrowth, she took the time to reflect on her" what ifs."

What if she had got another five-second start on them?

"I would have easily clawed back that blond animal, and by now, my kestrel talon would have it pinned to the ground, and my beak would be tearing its fur from its tiny body. It sure would have been a good start to my day."

As she lifted herself back into the skies, she needed to start hunting for her first meal again. As she flew back up, she reminded herself that there is always a next time! And now she had the two little things marked for the future, hopefully not too far away as she would like to taste something different. Something different would indeed be a nice treat sometime soon.

Now, Titch-Ella and Hoaby dare not fly, for if their new hunter saw them flying, there was no way they would get away from it. The kestrel hawks are real speedsters, and it was probably still around up there somewhere. So carefully, they started walking, one leading while the other watched the skies overhead. Yard by yard, they went down the hill and over the ditches. It was near sunset by the time they got down to the clan, who lived under the overhanging grass ledge on the edge of the river's gravel bank on the other side of the town. The area had been planted with trees and bushes as part of the town's park development for the townspeople to enjoy. It was the unlikeliest place to find a Lepralite clan group, being so close to many humans. But it all seemed to work for them. Maybe that is what is meant by the saying," hiding in plain sight." As they entered the dugout caves that broke into passageways that spread out under the park, they were met by an oddly familiar voice," Hey guysssss." it was Oddbod, Olden's butler. He was one of the most bizarre-looking Lepralites one could ever see, all dressed in his hippy-styled clothes of many colours. It was easy to see his birth happened too close to a flower bed, and with the poor lad unable to pronounce a simple S as it alwaysss ended up as many, everyone had to listen to him carefully when he talked so that he could be understood. However, he was also born with a crystal ball-like gift in his head that allowed him to see the immediate future. He was able to see who was coming and what they wanted. It was handy for any butler to be born with such gifts, as they would always know what their employer was looking for or wanted.

"Yousssss guysss are heresss to see Olden I guessss, I think itssss only Titch-Ella that can meet with him, assss itssss a ssssituation between himssss and hersss.

Hoaby felt he was being left out, which he was. But he had to accept that it was one of the Elders they came to see, and their wishes had to be respected. Titch-Ella followed Oddbod down the passageway, which felt like she was walking around forever sweeping corners, going around back on itself until they came to a doorway closed off by hanging dried long grass or rushes. Oddbod stopped and ushered her to go ahead into Olden's area. On pushing her way through the grass folds, she entered a bright room lit by the open void that looked out onto the river. She could hear the trickling waters pass as she stood waiting—nothing was in the room except what looked like a copper bath polished to reflect the orange light that distorted its mirroring. After waiting and walking in circles around the bath for some time she noticed the water in it beginning to bubble. Then it started whirling around like a upside down whirlpool that lifted Olden out of it, leaving the wetness to drain from his kilts as he hovered in mid-air above it. Titch-Ella noted he was not using his wings to keep himself in the air. Olden was looking like a dripping angel with closed eyes and clasped hands that were locked together.

Then POP!

His green eyes opened brightly, and his kilt was dispelling any of the age he carried, which now glistened as the air carried him away from the bath and lowered him to stand in front of Titch-Ella, who was left in amazement at his powers.

"Welcome, little one," he spoke calmly, with trust exuding from his words.

" Come, let us sit over here near the river." Strolling toward the open area, he said, "There is nothing like the waters of life to re-energize an old brain. Many times, I sit here looking at the river flowing on past. I often wonder what it would be like to be just one little drip of water swept along with all the other drips of water just following around the bends of the riverbank. Then pushed into a narrow point where we all would speed up, then it widens, and we all slow down. But I think if I looked at myself at the end of my journey down the river, I would see a very different me than I was when I first entered the stream."

Titch-Ella smiled as she sat on the earth floor. Oldens story led her mind into a place she was not used to, but she got the same feelings from him as when her Mum, Mrs. McCarthy, was talking to her, showing love, caring and wisdom, like when they were dressing the Christmas tree, or the time Mum explained to her how and why they had become so important to the family. There was something profound and caring in Olden that Titch-Ella connected with. Olden settled on the floor opposite her and stretched out both of his hands to allow her to take hold of them. The four hands cupped together, locking together like some premade jigsaw puzzle being completed.

"I told you the story of the river because it reminds me of my life. What I am about to show you I would like you to find understanding in it, please do not judge me too harshly."

"Now" Oddbod said "you were looking for Doadi?"

"Yes," she said, "Ma, our neighbour is carrying a lot of heartbreak, and I am hoping I can find this character who seems to me is the only one who can fix her sad feelings." Looking at Olden, she saw a tear trickle down his grey-haired cheek.

And he spoke, "Now, little one, close your eyes," she felt a jolt of electricity transferring from his hands to hers. Suddenly, like turning on a telly, the picture brightened to show a little girl peeling potatoes. Alongside her was a shining bright Lepralite with flowing green hair and blue eyes. Then the image flashed to a land of flames and a boy Lepralite crying out, "Floreen, Floreen." The pain that came with the picture was too unbearable for Titch-Ella to absorb. Then the image moved to two little Lepralites tucked together, rolled in a face cloth on what felt like an airing cupboard shelf. When the little male Lepralite opened its green eyes, Titch-Ella knew it was Olden's eyes. Then the pictures flashed to four Elders around a bath of bright water, with one of them stepping in, followed by the young Lepralite with orange hair and green eyes. The two disappeared down into the bright waters. Titch-Ella felt herself waiting for them to return from its depths, but only one returned. The young Lepralite was gone, only replaced by Olden. The only thing that did not change was his eyes as the rest of him transformed into the Elder that had accompanied him down into the bath of the bright waters.

Titch-Ella felt her connection to Olden broken as she sat back in thoughts of his past.

"Now, little one, you have seen who you have been looking for, and maybe now you can understand why Doadi had not returned to Margaret?"

From the past pictures the Elder had shown her, Titch-Ella understood why Doadi had not returned to Ma, for it would be impossible, as he had undergone the Lepralites highest honour by going through the transformation.

****

Her quest was over for now, but she still had many unanswered questions.

11. The Fox Dilemma

The animal food chain can be complex and twisted at times. Many factors can come into play, leaving the old food chain theory of humans at the top and a microbe at the other end of that chain not always true. We all heard the statement that people use, "eat or be eaten." I think that is a "human sentiment of silliness" for life is not that simple. We all know that some dogs will allow kittens to sleep next to them, but I know by watching a cat's reaction when they meet a strange dog. Their back goes up into an arch shape with fear, and they are ready to fight. Something buried in their makeup causes that reaction, leading one to think that dogs and cats have a dodgy history in the animal world. But they have both been conditioned over time by humans to live and interact with each other. However, if a wild dog met a wild cat, they probably would not ever be friends.

****

Geary was directly responsible for many chicken deaths in the area recently. He was the one who was teaching humans that their use of the words "free range "just meant "take away" for him. So much so that the local hens found themselves in security pens to keep them alive long enough to lay an egg. But now, Geary is forced to hunt for other food sources, or he will starve. The need for food will teach animals and humans alike that they need to learn new tricks if they are going to survive. Sometimes, Geary is seen in the town rummaging in bins when, an hour later, he would be running through the fields with a rabbit in his mouth. So, for a Lepralite to stand before him and discuss the merits of being more choosey about his diet or trying to explain why he should leave their friends alone was not an option if they wished to stay alive.

When something is as small as a Lepralite, it learns to

survive in its surroundings by being clever and using its small size to its advantage. By not going toe to toe with something bigger and stronger or even faster than they are, being of limited stature allows them to hide very well and to be quick and agile in small spaces. So, no open space conflict would be advised. Still, the most significant defense mechanism that a Lepralite inherited was their very clever brain. Titch-Ella had become a master of this, using her understanding of the animals' and other natures that lived around her, to get them to do what she wanted by using their trigger points, in the same way as a human would tell their child they would be left without good things such as ice cream or sweets if they continue to upset their parents. The trigger point is not having the ice cream or sweets given to them.

****

This story, crazy as it reads, is a case in point of how Titch-Ella uses these trigger points to get what she needs.

****

Still feeling sad, stressed, and tired and trying to work out the basic logic of Oldens water story about flowing down as part of a bigger river. But the only water she wanted right now was in Oldens bath and she just wanted to hop into it to get herself refreshed. She snuggled down into Adams's coat pocket, which hung in the hall cupboard away from all the McCarthy household annoyances such as Hoaby and Cody who had grated on her tired brain all day, Sometimes the world just got too much for her. Usually, her love would be spreading all about. But tonight was not one of those times; even the bats were testing her with their constant peeping noises,

" What do they want? Don't they know enough is enough already?" she thought, trying to snuggle down lower into her woolen, cosy space. But still, "peep peep," they persisted. By now, she felt she was a martyr to everybody's wants except her own and closed her eyes.

"Titch-Ella. Hello. Can you not hear we are wanted?"

It was Hoaby again annoying her; he pulled back the pocket flap,

" Come on. It's Suzy; she is in trouble," Hoaby shouted, panicked by his friend's lack of interest.

"Suzy who?" she asked wearily,

"Suzy, the squirrel, our old neighbour is in real trouble. She is trapped. Come on, let's go."

Within a millisecond, the fog lifted from Titch-Ellas's brain. Suzy was an orphaned squirrel who, just being only a kit young thing, had found herself alone in the back forest. Nobody knew how she had got there, but Titch-Ella had taken it upon herself to look after her and tried to teach the youngster some survival skills. Not being a squirrel herself, some of those lessons fell a bit short, but thank goodness Suzy met a mate who taught her some valuable lessons in the art of Squirrel Survival and storage of food, etc. That friendship did not last as one day he went gathering and never returned, leaving Suzy with little winter food and two small kits, young ones for her own to raise.

" OMG, where is she?" Titch-Ella asked, jumping out of the letterbox flap, trying to catch up with Hoaby, who did not answer her back as he was travelling urgently up towards the forest, flapping his wings as fast as he could, trying to follow the bats. Time felt like it was running away from them no matter how quickly they flew. They began to hear shrieking and hissing as they got closer to the trees, showing them at least the squirrel was still alive but very frightened. Reaching a large oak tree that the bats pointed out took a few minutes. Landing on its bark halfway up its trunk allowed the Lepralites to look down onto a dreadful situation where Geary was circling a squirrel and her two babies, which were cornered backed up against the bottom of the tree. It was obvious that they were trapped. Hoaby sprang into action, "I will fly down and distract him while you get Suzy out of here."

With that, he dropped off the tree and glided down and across the fox's eye line, but it did not blink or move its head. Hoaby flew back across again, getting dangerously close to the fox's pointed, jagged, flaring nostrils. However, still, it did not take its targeted focus away from the little red squirrel as he moved with menace in a semi-circle, waiting for the opportunity to pounce. Hoaby rested back next to Titch-Ella, who was looking around the forest floor for some inspirational wisdom to change the volatile situation.

"Look. It's Munchly. He will help," she said to Hoaby as she pointed down at a badger with his nose ruffling through the dead leaves and loose earth on the forest ground.

" Him! Are you joking? He wouldn't cross the road to help himself unless there were something in it for him, selfish git."

Hoaby was quite outspoken over Munchly's' selfishness!

Most badgers are loners anyway, but Hoaby did not understand that sort of animal, as he was very social. The irony of Hoaby's' lack of understanding of another animal's nature shows that he is just as self-centered as the badger.

" I'm going down to see if he will help," Titch-Ella said, dismissing Hoaby's guff.

"Good luck with that one," Hoaby called out after her. Looking down carefully surveying the situation on her glide groundward towards the busy badger.

Gently landing on its back in case she might spook him, she moved up towards his thick black and white head, still gnawing at the ground.

" Did you not see what the fox did?" she whispered in his ear.

"Ya," he grunted, not lifting his head. "Ya. He wants to eat the squirrels, but I'm too busy to get involved."

"NO. No, that's not important at all. You're right."

She tried to cross her fingers behind her back, which she did whenever she had to tell a big fib or white lie. But she needed to get the badger's help. Desperate times need desperate measures. And they were desperate now! As the hungry fox got closer to his prey, she knew she had to use what she knew to be his trigger point,

"Did you not see him grab and steal the worms before he saw Suzy?"

"WHAT worms?" his head was up now, and Titch-Ella had his full attention; his hair on his back stood straight up. "My worms, he is stealing my worms, my food. Him?"

"Oh yes," Titch-Ella replied. "I thought you allowed him to take them. How else would he have them hidden on his back?"

Now, we all know two things. One, that foxes don't eat worms, and two, he certainly would not hide them on his back. But this was all about triggers, which caused logic to be tossed aside. In this case, one. worm, two. pieces of food, and three. Stealing food that belonged to the badger, was put into Munchly's head, by a clever word twisting Lepralite lady. So, you can understand why the badger went nuts.

Geary was ready to attack. He could see the squirrels were tiring, and if he sprang now, he could take one of the small ones, and the mother would probably run up the tree. He needed to separate them quickly, not giving her time to bite him, as a squirrel had bitten him before and still had the scar on his nose. This time, he was going to handle them with care. Slowly, he moved in with laser-like eyes, targeting the little one on the outside. He knew the mother could not get across in time to shelter it.

Bit by bit, paw over paw, getting closer.

THEN...... WALLOP!

He rolled across the ground and lay flattened. He could not catch his breath. Something had hit him hard. Then he felt a stern nose lift and flip him into the air. On landing, he was dug again by the black and white hammer-like head pushing him around the ground like an old drink can, being kicked down the street. Titch-Ella jumped off Munchly's back and told Hoaby, who was on the ground by now, "to get some worms for the badger. There is plenty in the mud near the river. I think our friend deserves some treats." It was her way of apologising for coercing him into a situation he did not want to be part of. It did not take long for Hoaby to return with a fist full of worms for the badger. Somewhere in all the confusion of activities about the concerns of the babies' wellness and the badgers' state of mind, Geary, feeling very shaken and sore, had got up and limped away into the darkness.

When asked by Titch-Ella why the fox attack was able to happen, which left them so vulnerable, Suzy started crying," I was never thought to build up high, and I had made our nest in the old log ditch over there." She pointed out a rooted-out destroyed area of rotted logs. "I never saw a fox in these woods before." Titch-Ella put the whole near disaster down to Suzy's lack of experience as she had no parents to show her how to survive, and being such a young mother, the Lepralites still needed to help her some more, as there was no way they would survive out in the open.

" I have the perfect place for you and the little ones to be safe," Titch-Ella said as she waved a gesture for them to follow her." "Come before the fox returns," they left Munchly chewing his worms and headed back toward the McCarthy's Garden. Titch-Ella's mood was full of self-satisfaction as she looked over her shoulder to see the two little squirrels scurrying behind their Mum, all trying to keep up with her as they crossed the field. It was very early in the morning when they scrambled over the shredded hedge entwined with old, netted wire, getting into the McCarthy's back garden.

Hoaby landed on top of the birdhouse attached to the apple tree, "I believe this is going to be their new home."

"Yes, hopefully," his friend replied, "That is if they can fit through the holes; they seem very small. Looks like they were cut out only to fit small birds."

Suzy looked up at the two boxes and asked if they were really for them. Titch-Ella nodded.

" Oh, thank you so much, thank you."

Once more, the young squirrel's tears flowed with gratitude as she ran up the tree. Yes, the hole was too small. However, squirrels were born with two front teeth that would match any chisel, so she started to work. Then, the Cody alarm was activated, and he was on duty again. The lights in the bedrooms came on.

"Whoops! Now we are in trouble," Hoaby said, waiting for the back door to open and poor Cody to be shoved out. The two kitten squirrels hopped on the tree, climbing towards their busy mother.

The door opened, and out he bounded, barking up at the boxes. But this time, it was not Adam behind the dog but Mum,

" What's going on here? It's as busy as parade day, and it's only four-thirty in the morning."

Then, looking up, she saw a squirrel chewing into her new bird boxes. "What?" stunned by the cheek of the animal destroying her plans.

" Get out, go away, will you?" she shouted but was stopped by Titch-Ella's words,

" Mum, they have nowhere else to go, please?"

Mum was taken aback, and everything paused. Even Cody's barking stopped while waiting for Titch-Ella's explanation. Court was about to begin as the squirrels sat with Hoaby on a branch of the apple tree, waiting for Mum's judgment of Titch-Ella's story. Finally, after ending her account of the night's strange happenings, Mum agreed to lend the bird box to the squirrels even though she did doubt the story's authenticity. But for Mum, it was all about showing trust in Hoaby and Titch-Ella, so the squirrels returned to work creating their new entrance to their new home. On looking across the field, Mum asked,

"What is that? It sure is strange."

All eyes were drawn to a bright-looking orb of light moving toward them. Getting closer, it started to reveal itself in many colours as though it was a rainbow ball of fire. As the object approached, it massively increased as it hovered over the garden. Cody whimpered and hid behind Mum's legs, who was weak with fear, as she looked up at the strange whirling misty circle that covered the width of a brightly lit garden. Then changing shape to a funnel, pouring its dew down into a single point on the ground which kept twirling. The touch-down end began to sparkle lighter and brighter. It twirled down its dew until a small mass of firing sprinkled light condensed into one mass.

Then.

Puff!

As though touched by a magician's wand, there the Elder stood, glowing in all his finery with his glowing green and yellowed gold kilt, dark blue-grey draped hair, and the brightest green colour sparkling from his eyes. Olden stood there with his arms stretched wide, showing his cloaked wings. All were in awe of the power surrounding something so small. Titch-Ella and Hoaby felt they should be bowing down to a King. But he was not a King, nor would he want to be. He was a learned Elder, a Lepralite of wisdom who epitomised all that was balanced in our world. Mum felt as if she was drowning in his presence of goodness. She had never been in the company of such a mighty outpouring of beauty that wrapped around her. It was everything she would have prayed for, when she used to have her childhood dream many years ago. As the mist evaporated, Older lifted from the damp grass-covered ground to allow him to look straight into Mum's eyes. If there was ever a window to the soul, it was the unfiltered view that Mum had his heart, leaving her with a gentle, soft feeling inside as he began to speak to her.

"Oh Jane, the world has watched your kindness towards our animals over the years. You have always shown your beauty within, despite you trying so hard to hide it. Thank you and your family for taking Titch-Ella and Hoaby into your heart and home. I think you have a lot to teach them."

"Maybe they have a lot to teach us, too," Mum replied.

He smiled a gentle, elderly smile,

" Maybe."

He thought for a few moments. Mum could see his thoughts were drifting away from her as he paused for a moment. Then he started to speak even slower than before.

"Years ago, a little girl called Margaret was close to my brother. Now I am here to ask you to go to her and let her know that I am here and have a message from Doadi. Please be gentle with her; it will be a huge shock for her after so many years. Please, can you bring her here to me before the light rises and I must leave?"

" Yes, of course, I will go to her now." Mum returned to the cottage, and a few minutes later, her car was heard revving up the road towards Ma's home.

Olden turned to Titch-Ella and took her by the hand, saying,

" I know this morning that you are feeling good about yourself for rescuing your squirrel friend, but I will ask you that sometimes, you ask yourself, is what I am doing interfering with the balance of life? That is why we are here. We are here to keep balance in the cycle of life. Not to weight it our side, for then it is no longer balanced, A few years ago, I found a little fox cub. He was all on his own after some farmers had put poison on the land, and it had killed its mother and its sister.

" Oh, that is awful. Did he survive?" She asked.

"Yes, luckily" and he continued.

" Without my help, he indeed would have died. So, I took him to Mrs. Dunken, the Lord's wife, who bottle-fed him until he was old enough for dog food. The fried chicken was his favourite. When he was strong enough to survive in the wild, he left the farm and never came home. Yes, he was a beautiful little cub, and Mrs. Dunken named him in honour of her Dad's name."

He paused.

"What was it he called him? Yes. She called him Geary! If I had never rescued him, many chickens would still be alive, and your friend would still be living in the woods, but still, I am glad I saved the little cub. Do you see, my girl, life is not always as black and white as we would like it to be!"

A car pulled up outside, and two doors had opened and closed. The squirrels had made their way into their new home, and the three Lepralites were sitting on the old outside table the gardeners had found and brought to the McCarthy's garden to cheer it up. It was now less than half an hour before sunrise. Mum entered the garden and walked towards the Lepralites. Olden's eyes were fixed on the back door, waiting for Margaret to come through them. Each second that passed gave him more time to get more nervous. He could feel the memories of a little girl bubbling in his little thumping heart. How could he ever explain to her why he could not come back here? Then, she stepped through the doorway with her pink cardigan over her knee-length skirt and flat shoes. With her moving closer to him, he could see through the many layers of past years to that little girl on the inside. How will she accept the truth? Still trying to choose his word to explain it all to her, she stopped, put on her glasses, and stooped down to look at Olden. On seeing his bright green eyes, she cried out.

" Doadi, is it you? Oh lord God, thank you for returning him to me."

Her tears ran freely down her face.

" Little Margaret. Please. Yes. It is me, but only some of me. It's hard to explain, but yes, Doadi is here."

But Ma was not listening, for she had seen Doadi's eyes. And he knew she would not accept or understand even if he could share the Lepralites' secrets. To become an Elder, Doadi had to transfer over himself to revitalise and become part of the ageing Elder, for an Elder comprises of many of the best-chosen Lepralites.

"My Doadi. I missed you so much. I miss Floreen so much. I'm so sorry Dad killed her."

The pain started to flow from her mouth.

" I have prayed that I would get the chance to look for your forgiveness. I know when you lost your partner, you cannot live alone. I'm so sorry we killed you both."

Olden walked across the table and held his hand for her to take hold of it.

"Nobody killed Floreen. The fire took her, and nobody could have predicted the wind would blow the fire in the direction it did. Floreen was only doing what she knew, saving vulnerable animals. I still see her whenever I look at our stars as she sparkles down on us. And for me, I am still here. I might not look the same as the young thing you knew back then."

She smiled at his quirk on what age did to them both.

" Little Margaret. You need to know you have always had our love; we are just sorry we did not see our little girl grow into the beautiful person you now are today."

Ma's heart was breaking with sorrow and release from the years of pain she had carried as her tears kept weeping.

"Will I ever see you again?"

"Every night, my little Margaret. Every time you look up.'

He pauses.

" Only if there are not too many clouds or rain."

He smiled again. He raised his arms and disappeared in a burst of gusted breeze, leaving Ma with her thoughts of the days that once were and the wondering fear of never seeing him again.

****

12. Wood or Carrier Pigeon?

The whole month had been clammy.

The weather was passing off another soft wet spring and was now dragging itself towards the summer's arrival with the last few days showing the sun.

Ma lay alone on her super king size bed which dwarfed her bedroom space. She knew it was disproportionate to the rest of the middle-sized room, but it was one of the few luxuries she allowed herself after her husband had passed away only two years earlier. She knew his quirky sense of humour would find her extravagant bed hilarious, for when he was alive, they had slept in a bed barely more than four feet wide and as plain as pancakes. Whenever he talked about getting a larger bed, she would tell him that it was not needed as there were only the two of them in it, and he only ever used eight inches of the mattress, because he was so scrawny!

But the real reason was that she had nursed him for the last three years of his life, and there was no room for a large bed along with all the medical machines that had cluttered the room.

She was laying back on her many cushions that adorned her bed resembling a queen of the cush. This time of the night allowed her to stop thinking about all the trials of her day along with all the mysteries of who was doing what to who in her local area. It was mind blowing just how much she needed to think about. However, others would think most of the challenges that perplexed her mind had absolutely nothing to do with her. But that was not the way Ma looked at life. Generally mistrusting human behaviour, she found it much easier to manage situations and the people around her, to keep her own status quo, allowing her to live in her more balanced content environment.

Tonight, however, she found herself wrestling with that one fancy cushion that she loved to look at. However, the stuffing in it was not as cosy as it looked. It was stiff in the middle which shoved a knot of wool into her soft shoulder as she tried to read her glossy woman's magazine. She had picked one up that day in the local shop, Again, though, not much had changed in all those years of buying them. In her opinion, the young models were still pretty little things, and the dresses were still full of glam, none of which she coud see herself wearing; however, she did think that some of the colours exhibited in this month edition would give her some ideas of what was in fashion, as she did have her daughter's wedding to look forward to in the coming months.

Tic Tic Tic

" What is that noise?" She thought.

Tic Tic Tic

"It sure is annoying."

But she continued to scan the page in front of her, then she heard her cat begin to shout off.

"Meow," in its screeching high-pitched groan.

" Oh, for goodness' sake. Is there no rest for me tonight? I had better see what's going on."

Again.

Tic Tic Tic

On and on.

"What the blazes is that?"

She laid down the magazine on the duvet, took the spectacles off her nose leaving them hang on her neck chain and sat up. She swung her legs out of the bed and stuffed her feet into her favourite, once fluffy pink slippers, grabbed her dressing gown from the end of the bed and went out onto the landing and flicked on the lights, calling out" Who is there"?

She was mindful that she was on her own in the house as

her daughter was staying over in the city.

Again.

Tic Tic Tic

Looking down towards the front door at the end of the hallway, she could see her cat clawing at the woodwork trying to get out. She began her frumpily hurriec way, stepping down towards the door,

"I swear to the Lord himself. If that cat has messed up again… fifteen hundred euros of uselessness,"

She felt every step down was an effort,

" What's wrong with you, Digger. Have you forgotten where your cat flap is ya duff?"

She paused to look around "Oh, sorry pet. I must have closed the kitchen door on my way to bed." She felt a hot flush come over her." So sorry, my brain is not what it was."

She opened the door to the kitchen and her cat took off in the direction of the back door and its flapping exit. Ma followed him towards the back of the room. Before she opened the door, with only reasons known to herself, she picked up one of her large baking rolling pins and stepped out into her back garden.She could now clearly hear the sharp tic tic tic coming from her back bedroom window above her head. The bright moonlit night allowed her to see a pigeon perched on the sill with its beak tapping on the glass,

"What the blazes are you up to?" she called up at the bird who turned and at once glided down semi flapping its wings as it landed on the ornate concrete railings next to her.

" That's strange for a wood pigeon" she thought as she could see it was carrying a small material made message pouch around its leg.

" Blooming heck, are we back in the dark ages or something?"

Strangely, the bird stood still when she pulled the bit of paper out. On opening it she could see something written on it, but she had to lift her specs back on her nose again. Using the light from the house she read.

" K can you come get me."

Still a bit flabbergasted by the strangeness of it, she began to question who she knew that had initials of K? The only person that came to her mind was young Katie, who lived in the house behind her.

Still confused," who would send a message like this? "What time is it?"

She raised her watch.

It was 11.05pm.

"No, it is too late to ring the McCarthy's now."

Then, thinking some more she had a Ding moment.

" The only person who would produce such a hair brained idea would be Dickey Dunken. But how am I to know it's him? He won't give out his phone number, so I don't have it, but Katie has been spending a lot of time at his farm and the K could be for her as the paper was very small so he could not write Katie. Yes. that must be it."

Again, Ma has found herself looking after the

neighbourhood. Despite Dickey Dunkens' unwelcoming attitude towards humans, she thought she had better go and look.

But this was pushing t, even for Ma.

Now fully dressed and mission bound - "watch, wallet, mobile phone, handbag and my car keys, I am ready to go" she thought as she closed the front door on her way to the car. Looking at her watch again, now it was just past eleven thirty pm.

" Am I mad? What if he is OK and he starts hurling abuse at me? Ya, but what if he is dying? Ok, I am going to risk it."

She turned the key, revved the engine, and drove down the laneway and swung back into the farm's long tree covered tunneled driveway. She could see the old house at the end of the dark lane. All was quiet. It gave her an eerie feeling, as though she was back in her childhood. Old farmhouses had left a stain on her memories. She refused to ever go back to her father's old place once she married Johnny, as it carried too many dark memories. The demise of her Lepralite friends was always front and center in her mind. However, also the passing of her Mum when Ma was so young, followed by the Cinderella treatment she received from her brothers and father were etched deep within her.

To put it mildly, big old farmhouses were not her favourite places, especially in the middle of the night.

She stopped her car in front of the dreary sad-looking house.

She could see no lights on. However, the big old side gate rattled against the side wall of the house, telling her the farm was open. That was not normal even for Dickey Dunken's strange ways.

She started her car again and drove around into the back paddock. The moon still shone brightly as she stepped nervously from her car.

"Mr. Dunken," she called out.

The large old black shed door was open and moving ever so slightly back and forth in the light breeze squeaking as it did so.

" Something is most definitely wrong" she thought, as she stood not straying from the safety of the car.

"Mr. Dunken, are you there?"

She listened but could only hear the ghostly sounding door.

Then she heard "Help, is somebody out there?"

It was a man's fainted whispered cry out. She closed the car door and began with her disorganised handbag swinging jog towards the shed. She slipped in between the two doors. The dim light hanging from the ceiling allowed her to see a set of legs and a walking stick on the floor behind the large bench in the center of the floor,

" Oh no, Mr. Dunken are you ok?"

The elderly man was lying on his side. Ma could tell he was in a lot of pain as he was gripping his walking stick handle so tightly it showed his white knuckles, and a lone tear sat on his face.

"I fell when checking on the animals, I think I must have broken my hip, but I will be ok,"

"I do not think you will be ok, Mr. Dunken. I need to call an ambulance."

She pulled her mobile phone from the bottom of her bag and started to call for the emergency services. Mr. Dunken tried telling her to stop making a fuss, that he wanted to stay with his animals, and he would be fine. But he still could not get off the floor, just wincing with pain when he tried.

He moved again,

"Lie still will you," she exclaimed in a commanding manner, then went back talking on her phone giving directions. It was a long-drawn-out conversation as the area was remote to any city folk and she had no post code to give. When finished she turned her attention back to the retired farmer who was asking her "Why are you here Ma? Not that I am not happy to see you, but why are you here in the middle of the night?"

"Mr. Dunken. I would be at home, in my bed, except for some crazy pigeon who came knocking on my window, and around his leg there was some encrypted message. I started thinking, who it might be from? and the only one around here that would send a bird with a message is you, you crazy old goat. Am I right?"

The old man smiled, "so they made it then? Well, they, I mean he nearly got there. He was supposed to go and wake Katie."

Ma could tell he was full of pride for having such a clever idea. But she just started shaking her head in disbelief,

" You really are a crazy old man."

Between his discomfort and his neighbours overwhelming

orderly manner, he took a moment to gather up his next sentence,

"Maybe so, but at least I got your attention when I fell. I had no phone, but Steamer our pigeon landed near me, and seeing as Katie was trying to train the bird to be a carrier pigeon and fly to her house and back with messages, well, it was the only way I could get attention."

Ma did not believe him but wanted to keep him awake by talking to him until the ambulance arrived.

"You said Katie was training the wood pigeon to be a carrier pigeon? That is a bit much,"

"Maybe so" he muttered, "but the bird must have got a bit lost. He is not the brightest, but he has a big heart. Well, that is what Katie thinks anyway."

Ma found herself smiling as she listened to him speak of his pigeon as though it was human. But she gave him grace as she had a life full of strange happenings too.

Mr. Dickey Dunken was, in his own words, a self-professed hermit. He found life to be less complicated having little or no humans around him. He had given up on most, for their lack of interest in the native wild animals of Ireland of which he cared so deeply for. He had no interest in trying to educate or convince people who were more interested in helping with issues word wide, instead of a few native species of animals that were now disappearing from the Irish landscapes. He held a high brow cynical attitude to the many who would try telling him that he was for the birds. He would simply reply saying" yes, of course I am, and I am for the rest of the animals that need our help too,"

He knew people were trying to mock his thought patterns as he did not hold theirs. He would choose to stop a debate before a discussion was needed. His relenting bludgeoned stay away attitude worked, leaving him with little or no visitors, and that suited him just fine, until a young lady and her Mum drove down his driveway early one morning bringing back one of his rare barn owls, who he had named Donut.

Her name was Katie McCarthy, a young bright-eyed eleven-year-old that now had turned twelve. She had black curling hair and dark brown caring eyes, which seemed to have drilled into the old mans hardened heart. She had become the granddaughter he never had or was it the joy that she could not help herself showing when she was around the animals. In a very short space of time, young Katie had brought hope back into his heart. He could see with a little teaching she could take up the mantle of wild animal protection just like children had done in other parts of the country. But Katie had one huge insight that other children or teenagers did not have. That was the help and teachings from the Lepralite community as did Dickey Dunken. Being a bachelor and having Snizzel and Albie staying with him in the big house, somehow it all worked well as they were all somewhat outsiders and as odd as each other in different ways.

Snizzel, who was a sufferer of hay fever, struggled with conversation as he was not used to them due to his lack of friends who had got on with playing and living life to the fullest without him, when he could not be out and about in the pollen filled air.

Albie, he was a pure albino Lepralite that had huge problems being out in the sunlight.

But by understanding each other's needs and space, the living arrangement seemed to work very well.

Except for the night Mr. Dunken ended up lying on the floor with a broken hip and nobody around to help as his two-house mates were off celebrating this month's High Moon.

The part of Dickey Dunken's story that Ma found hard to believe, all started when Katie brought Titch-Ella and Hoaby to the farm to meet up with Snizzel and Albie as she knew how important it was for Lepralites to socialize often to revitalize each other. The spring had brought a strong sun which was not allowing Albie to venture out much and the raised pollen content in the air was also causing problems for Snizzel.

Katie had found her Mums old, styled ladies' bike in the shed. As it had a front carrier basket it was perfect for taking the little ones with her. It was well set up with a crumpled-up scarf giving both comfort and if needed, a hiding place for Titch-Ella and Hoaby in case anyone was curious enough to investigate the basket. This day Katies enthusiasm to get down to the farm quickly found her peddling full pelt into the paddocks. But this time, a plump pigeon sat plop in the middle of the square. As the bicycle approached it did not stir.

"Move" Katie shouted, "I cannot stop."

Yet there was no response from the bird. Thinking quickly, she pulled on the handlebars steering the bicycle around the grey bird and in through the open black barn doors and skating all the way to the back into a pile of straw which cushioned their stop. She quickly lifted the bike up.

"Are you guys, ok?" She lifted the scarf to check cn her passengers but there was nobody inside the basket.

"Oh no" she exclaimed, "I have lost you two."

" No, you didn't," A voice came from over her head. Katie looked up and saw the two little ones sitting on the large timber beam.

Hoaby, who had a big mischievous grin on his face, said "Katie, you really are a bad driver" but before she could answer Mr. Dunken defused her self-frustration,

"Oh, I see you met Steamer our pigeon. He is not too bright when it comes to traffic. As a matter of a fact, I don't think he is bright about anything."

Katie looked out the barn door to make sure that it was all right, but it still had not moved from its spot as it calmly pecked between the old cobble stones on which it rested.

"Don't mind Mr. Dunken," a voice came from under the old bench. On looking down she could see the all-white Lepralite,

" He is quite clever; Steamer I'm talking about."

Katie smiled, "H Albie, what are you doing down there?"

She could see he was trying to sow some material together, but the needle was big and awkward for him to handle.

"Can you help me do this Katie? I am trying to make a little pouch so that Steamer can carry his messages in it,"

" That is a good idea." But then she thought for a moment,'

But is Steamer not just a wood pigeon?"

Albie put down the needle and thread on the floor and flew up onto the bench top so to be closer to her level of sight. Katie knew how he acted, and that he needed to tell her one of his very detailed educated styled stories that he was well known for. To which she had already experienced while conversing with him on various topics that he wished to discuss.

"It is not so simple. Yes, to look at him you would think he is a wood pigeon, being so plump or rounded in stature. I thought that when I first met him. But as I got to know him better, he told me in confidence that he wanted to be a racing pigeon. Now most would have laughed at that statement, but I could not, as I knew what it felt like to be mocked. But I also knew he would never have the speed or the agility of a racing bird. But he reminded me that we can all be anything we wanted to be, within reason. And I had to agree with his statement, for I always wanted to be a flight fixer and despite my white handicap, I worked inside and worked hard and reached my goal. Now Lepralites come from all over Munster to get their wings realigned by me. So, who was I to tell him that he had to stay and be a wood pigeon just because it was that brand of egg he came from."

"You really are a very clever Lepralite. That is such clever thinking," Katie interrupted but then paused to let him continue.

" We discussed a lot of pros and cons of racing and came up with the idea that his time would be much better spent training to become a carrier pigeon as there were so few birds working this job now. It would be a much easier to get work."

Katie was dismayed by his logic despite his reasoning having a few quirks in it such as everybody has a mobile phone these days!

And, if he ever were to become a carrier pigeon, it would take years of training. But like Albie, she too was not going to break any hearts by arguing out the practicalities and realities of life in the modern age, that had little want for pigeons not to mind a carrier pigeon.

"Where do we start?" she asked Albie. "First, we need to make the carrier bag and attach it to his leg. Can you help me with that Katie?"

Not having her phone with her to check up on googles explanation of the makings of a carrier pouch for birds, she had to rely on her memory of watching an old musketeer movie where it showed carrier pigeons delivering messages to a queen's chamber maid. Despite not having any leather, she went to work with the same zest as though she was making a foiled Christmas star for her Mum's tree. It did not take her long until her little project was made and ready to attach.

" Now Albie, here you go," as she handed over the little pouch. "You had better put it on him as I do not think he will allow me especially after me nearly running him over today,"

"I think he was far more interested in the loose seeds on the ground than your bicycle."

He took the little bag and called out his bird call. Katie watched as the bird toddled into the barn and stood before Albie. She looked up at the beam to see if Titch-Ella and Hoaby were watching but they were gone as was Mr. Dunken.

"Again, I must have lost control of my minutes. That always happens when I start doing something," she thought to herself.

"They have all gone to the big house,"

"Sorry," she replied "Hobs and Titch. They have gone with Mr. Dunken. I heard something about cakes on offer."

Katie was surprised by his ability to read her mind, but he told her that he saw her looking at the beam for them. She gave a brief laugh at herself and her silly thinking, then asked," How are we going to train him?"

He seemed to have it all worked out, by his quick response" I will tell him, and you can show him."

She looked a bit confused, but just kept watching as he kept speaking in the wallowing and gerbiling language as he fitted the bag around the bird's leg. Then he stood up and rubbed his head against the pigeons' neck feathers and whispered again some weird gobbling words. Then he looked up at Katie,

"He is ready to fly now Katie. You must get on your bicycle and cycle to the entrance gateway. Then stop and Steamer will fly down to you, circle and then fly back to me here.

Everything was ready to go. Katie started to peddle off down the long lane towards the gate and sure enough the bird took off flying above her. When she stopped the bird circled over her twice and headed back towards the barn. It took a few minutes for her to get back and jump excitedly off her bike.

" That was amazing. Well done guys. Can we do that again?"

Steamer strutted around the barn floor. For the first time in his life, he had felt proud of himself. She knew how he felt, remembering the time she won her schools writing competition. She watched him stride out and Albie saying, "well done my flying friend." They waited until the b rd finished absorbing his triumphant moment. Then Albie went back to the bird and like the last time rubbed his head against the birds' neck and spoke in gobble tongues. Once again, he looked up at Katie.

"Now this is going to be a bit harder as you need to cycle home to your house and Steamer will stay over your head until you get there. Then he will circle and fly back."

But this time Katie went off in one direction and the pigeon in the other. When she saw he was not following her she went back to the shed and waited. It was at least thirty minutes before the bird returned. When the bird landed, he felt lost and angry with himself, but again Albie turned the birds' failings into a win.

"Yes! you needed to practice flying with the bag. Well done my friend, great flight."

The bird lifted his beak from the ground and once more began to strut. Katie turned to Albie and said, "you should have been a teacher."

He smiled "if I were a teacher I would be always in trouble, as I would insist on showing everybody all the wrong ways in order to show them how great it feels to get it right."

She smiled again" I still think you would be a wonderful teacher, regardless of what you think... Can we do some more training tomorrow? I want so much for him to find success.

The training sessions lasted several days until they all got it right. The pigeon flew all the way to Katie's bedroom window, tapped on it and flew back again to Albie in the barn. They were all excited about the bird's progress. Even Mr. Dunken found himself apologising to the bird for underestimating him.

Now even the moon began to celebrate, showing its fullness. Yes, that time of the month was here again.

For now, the stage was now set for a night of song with dance for some, a broken hip for another, and a distant friend picking up some pieces of her past.

****

13. Rainbows and Bobett

Evenings meant solitude for him.

Ever since he was a young Lepra, he had always looked forward to the darkness cloaking over his world, giving him a place to think of the days that could have been and to dream of what tomorrows could hold. With this time of year, he found his days dragging out and his darkness delayed. Dickey Dunken had set up the smallest room in the farmhouse to be a clean room for Snizzel. Its walls, ceilings and even floors were covered with some sort of white plastic covered board that one would normally find as a backing in a kitchen cupboard. Mr. Dunken had even covered the back of the large old door in the whiteboard and put draft seals around it to stop the microbes or dust entering the clean air sanctuary. The small window had blackout blinds fitted to keep the splinters of light out, as the brightness would stop the little thing from sleeping.

When Snizzel first saw the room that his friend had prepared for him, the sterile blandness scared him. But besides having an air purifier in the room, Mr. Dunken had put in a leather chair. Then he placed a tall timber narrow table which was a potholder in its last life. On it he sat a small dog's bed with a soft leather wrapped cushion for which the little lad could rest. Then came the greatest present in Snizzel little life - A remote-controlled wall projector. That was there to break any loneliness that he might ever feel. With the pictures bouncing off all walls or ceilings and with the inbuilt sound bar pushing out its vibrations around the room, it was the closest thing to reality that he could ever have imagined. Dickey Dunken had also, in his delightful old wisdom, plugged a music player into the system and uploaded some of his old songs and video collections to keep the Lepralite amused. With the chair in the cleanroom, they could both enjoy movie nights together. The room was clean, functional, and homely as much as it could be, and allowed Snizzel to fill his little vulnerable lungs with clean air.

Now he lay stretched out on his bed with thoughts full of worry. It was very lonely when Mr. Dunken was not hobbling around the place. Even though Albie was there, he was normally preoccupied with one or two of his wild brain wave ideas that always kept him away from having conversation or mixing in any way with Snizzel. Now, it was just the two of them alone in the big old house. Well, them and the group of squatters in the attic. It was different when Dickey Duncen was about, as he had always found ways for the three of them to be interacting. Whether it was as simple as doing the dishes after their meals together or working on some barn or farm project that they found themselves doing. But, for now, the linchpin of the family was in hospital getting hip replacement.

He stood up and jumped on the remote control a few times until he found his friends favoured old tune. Then he lay back to watch the projector disperse light across the ceiling. It formed a rainbow from one side of the room to the other and the song started as he closed his eyes to relax into the music, "Somewhere over the Rainbow, Blue Birds Fly..............."

His thoughts drifted back to the burrow of his birth, to a time when he was left crawling around on the dried grass floor coughing and gasping for breath, but then being picked up by his little purple-haired Lepra friend. She was the chubbiest of all the little Lepras. With her short little arms and big wings, she seemed all out of proportion except for her bright brown eyes. Maybe that is why her heart seemed to be twice the size compared to the rest of the sack batch. But by the time the birthing hole opened, she had grown into a stunning looking Lepralite. She caught the attention of many who were more dashing, stronger, and better coloured than poor Snizzel. Despite the burrow being a dark pollen filled pit of horrors for him, he often wished he was back there with her.

He began to picture a world of honey cups and candy floss just like the movies had shown him, where he could hold his friends' hand and slalom up and down on the curved rainbows in his room hugging with her as they waved the evenings away without a care in the world. But again, his eyes were open to the reality of a finished song and a blank wall with his wish seeming far away.

Not long after that baby Lepra burrow opened to the light, she was named Bobett by the Elders and then was paired off with a young strong brightly coloured Lepralite called Chipper. He was full of enthusiasm for life. Soon he was talking of showing Bobett a whole new world, and he took her away from the town's clan shortly after their naming. Despite asking the Elders many times what became of them, Snizzel was never able to get any information. He always asked the out-of-town clan members who travelled in for the moon celebrations, but none had ever heard those names. He felt that she was most definitely still alive as he would have felt the loss of connection to her, the same way he had when two of his sack batch Lepras went to Never Never Land, after they were run over by a speeding human's car last year. It was a horrible feeling for him as a shuddering pain shot through his body, and he fell to the ground unconscious. It was not until Mr. Dunken had spoken to one of the clan Elders about Snizzel having fallen on the floor for no apparent reason and how he would not wake up for three days, that he found out, all the other Lepralites born of the same sausage sack batch, had the same side effect. Just one more thing that a human had learned about the connections of these strange creatures. But for now, Snizzel's dream could still become a reality as if she was out there somewhere. He closed his eyes to rest and sleep overtook his thoughts.

The morning was brought to everybody's attention with Katie yelling,

" Wake up sleepy heads. "

She stood in the large hallway at the foot of what used to be the grand sweeping stairway, which once upon a time would have allowed three abreast to walk up or down it together. But today it was just an old, wasted space with worn handrails and a matted stairway that should be refitted, as the carpeting looked like it was dragged from a nineteen seventy's catalogue with its sunken inlayed cerise pink patterns and awful patched sun bleached, foot worn pink nylon wool, that was all too often fixed on with nails that belonged to a butcher. Looking up to the high corniced ceilings above the generations old paint work prompted Katie to want to explore, for she had never experienced such a large house. But that would have to wait for a while as Mum had asked her to attend to the few animals that still wandered around Dickey Dunken's farm as she and Adam were going up to the city hospital to visit him. And with Ma minding Clive for the few hours, it was left to Titch-El a, Hoaby and herself to carry out the tasks that were set for them and she did not want to let anybody down, especially Mr. Dunken.

"Hello! It's Saturday. Come on. Get up. Birds and animals need to be fed."

She looked down the long hallway which ran through the house to the kitchen at the end. All the doors were open leaving little hidden from sight. Each room was more outdated than the last. As she looked around, she noticed her two friends were gone.

"They have probably gone to find Snizzel and Albie,' she thought, but that gave her little peace of mind as the long passageway was making her uneasy with its disproportionate narrowness and high ceilings. It gave her a feeling that she was walking down a hill of no return. Then she entered the wide-open kitchen which had windows both facing the back paddocks and front ones to the driveway. On one wall sat what looked like a large wood burning cooker with clothes drying rack overhead and near it was a cream-coloured ceramic trough-styled sink with old ceramic taps that belonged in a bathroom. There were no counter tops that one would expect to see. Only a big open pine press where the plated cups and food boxes sat. Next to it standing all alone was a small fridge looking totally out of place showing off its whiteness. A large pine table sat in the middle of the floor with a chair either end, with a bench seat set back against the old wall some distance away.

" Oh no, who did that?"

Katie winced in horror as she saw bird feathers and little dirty claw prints stamped across one of the chairs with even a few on the table.

She called out, "Steamer, is that you? Mum will kill you. Well, she will get really cross with you anyways."

There was silence with no sign of any pigeon.

"Maybe, it was not him". She picked up a smelly damp cloth from inside the sink and started to clean the chair and table.

" We cannot find Albie anywhere."

It was Hoaby.

"I have been though the whole house. I even checked the attic, and the bats have not seen him either. If he went during the night they would have noticed. That is not like him. He will be burnt to a crispy crunch if the sun catches him outside."

Katie finished the wipe down and threw the cloth across the room back into the sink trough.

"Good shot," Hoaby shouted, but her mind was elsewhere.

" Come on. We had better find Albie. Where is Titch-Ella?"

"She went outside in case he is in the shed," he promptly replied but with that Titch-Ella flew into the kitchen.

"We have a problem. Steamer is missing. He never went back to the barn last night."

Katie was trying to slow her breathing to show the little ones that there was nothing to panic about, but inside her brain was in turmoil with all sorts of negative outcomes running though her mind.

Calmly she asked, "where is Snizzel?"

"He is resting. He had a bad night's sleep last night," Hoaby replied.

Katie sat down on the damp chair and thought that" at least that is one is accounted for."

Then she said.

"We need to come up with a plan guys. First, we need to feed the animals, and we can hope when we are doing that, they will come back. But in the meantime, we need to ask the crows for their help."

She turned to the little ones and asked,

" Titch-Ella, will you call them and explain the situation and

Hoaby and I will start feeding the birds in the barn,"

"And Snizzel?" Hoaby asked.

"Leave him sleep. He can catch up with us later if he wishes to. Come on. Let's get to it." Katie got up and followed her two little friends back down the hallway, which now had become just one more route out of the house. Her mind was now fully on a picture of a little albino Lepralite that could be burning up in the sunlight somewhere out in the big open world.

She kept trying to keep her thoughts on the jobs facing her, trying to remember where the various bags of seeds were. From watching Mr. Dunken when he feed the different birds in the barn, some scattered on the ground for the chickens and others were placed on high shelves for the owls and pigeons. She felt Hoaby land on her shoulder as she walked. Then she opened the side gate. She understood it to be his way of showing her that he is there for her, but neither spoke to the other as they walked towards the large black barn door at the back of the paddocks. She knew it would take effort to pull it open, so it came as a surprise to find it slightly open.

"That's strange," she thought as she passed through it. Hoaby lifted away from her to go up to the rafters still wanting to keep his distance away from the two owls, knowing how damaging they could be to his health!

Katie called out.

" Donut"

Then

"Cupcake"

But nothing happened.

She could see six or seven chicken coming her way so she closed the door quickly, and started counting them for there should be ten and a cock somewhere.

"One, two, three…,"

"Yes! At least they are all here. Thank goodness, I don't need to explain to Mr. Dunken that we have lost a chicken or two, especially after hearing the Lepralites stories of the fox Geary."

She took the corn seeds and shook them out on the ground for the chickens to peck on. And then she turned her attention back to the owls or lack of them more like!

"Can you see them Hoaby?" she called up to him.

"No, they are not up here, but they could be anywhere."

Then he lowered his voice.

" Normally we only see them when it's too late,"

"What did you say?" she asked again.

"No, they are not up here," he shouted back.

Then he flew back down to her.

"We have a big problem don't we Katie? No Donut, No Cupcake or Steamer and No Albie."

"Big problem indeed, and the barn door open and … Mum is going to kill me. I need help. But nobody is around. How can I even look for help, who would believe me anyway, about a missing thing that nobody knows exists and two barn owls and a plump pigeon that nobody cares about? God even Cody is not here."

She could feel her tears begin to flow down her face as she felt she had failed everyone, especially Mr. Dunken. But also, her Mum who had trusted her to look after the house and farm.

"Maybe, I still am only a child?" she thought.

Titch and Hoaby stood on the big bench next to her,

"Don't cry Katie. We will get this sorted," Titch-Ella said in her calming motherly loving voice. "The crows are gone looking for Albie and Steamer and the two owls have probably been out hunting and are not back yet. It is still quite early in the morning."

The clip clop of hooves was heard outside.

Then a rattle on the door.

Katie ran and opened it. She had forgotten about the donkey and his friend, the little Shetland pony, who were pushing their noses against the door looking for food.

" Oh no, I forgot about you two and I still need to feed the goats."

She felt she was drowning in all the work that needed to be done. Yet there was so little to do, as it was a place that took very little looking after compared to a normal working farm. But for the twelve-year-old, it felt the world was on her young shoulders.

But bit by bit she found herself working through her jobs and her anxiety starting to ease, with everything now running smoothly. Except for the odd tug of her coat and some nibbles that one of the cheeky goats gave her, it all went to plan with the hay and food pellets all distributed the way she had been shown. Now it was time to get back and solve the riddle of Albie and the missing birds. The hour of feeding had given her brain time to cool and the little one's time to chat with the animals around the farm which resulted in bits of information being gathered which did need tying together, the way actors did during the detective programmes on the TV.

The three gathered at the bench once again to pool all the stories together.

Titch was first to begin.

"From talking to the other pigeons, we know that the owls left about ten last night through the open vent window and that Steamer went over to the big house with Albie in the late afternoon and they were both in the kitchen for some time."

"Yes" Hoaby jumped in." But the sparrows who were messing around with their nests at the time, also told me something very weird about Albie. They said he was acting even more strangely than he normally did. He was mixing Mr. Dunken's grease with some white paint. But it was not working, and he was giving out about it. But he then took some bailer string and some grease back to the big house with him."

Katie was confused.

"How would he even carry such a thing and where are the two items? I did not see any grease around the house. However, the feathers and claw marks I cleaned off the kitchen seat must have belonged to Steamer and yes there were bits of sting on the table, but I thought nothing of it at the time. But where is the greasy paint? This quandary is getting weirder by the minute," she thought.

"We need go back to the big house and see if we can find the stuff that is missing," Katie surmised but her thoughts were disrupted by Hoaby adding "the sparrows could be telling fibs. Do you remember the time they were accusing the little birds of stealing their nesting material? I mean give me a break. Who would be stealing their nesting mud and twigs!"

Titch-Ella stopped his rant" Whether they did or did not, that would take some imagination to come up with a story like Albie was mixing grease with paint. No. I think they must be telling the truth. But why would Albie want grease?"

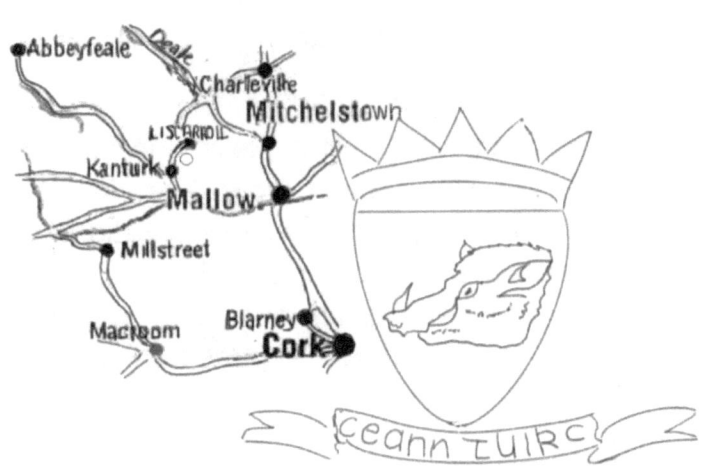

The scuttle of wings could be heard overhead as a dirty Donut and Cupcake came back through the open roof window and settled on their perch. Hoaby jumped behind Katie and peeped up from behind her as they all watched the birds fluff their specked feathers to settle and begin to close their eyes. Titch-Ella flew skyward towards the roof rafters with a bowl full of questions, but Katie was first to shout up,

"Did you guys see Albie and Steamer? We cannot find them anywhere."

Donut opened one eye and started twitting, shrieking, and purring like he was talking some cross language between a pigeon and a cat.

The little ones listened.

Hoaby was first to speak, "The birds said Albie is mad."

"Is that it?" Katie asked, "is that all they had to say?"

"Oh, something about Albie covering himself in grease and he kept slipping off Steamers back. But I do not know what else he was saying as he was talking too gurgled for me to hear properly."

"Is that it?" Katie asked again.

"Something about that the pigeon is mad too. He thinks he is a flying horse or something like a unicorn or such like! Wait for Titch-Ella to come and explain, but I do think, they know where they are."

Still the chatter kept going between the owls and Titch-Ella on the overhead beams. Katies impatience in looking for answers kept her looking up. She was watching one bird chatter and when it stopped the other started with Titch every so often saying something using a language which was not of any human tongue that she had heard spoken before. Still, she waited in anticipation. Until finally, the two owls closed their penny shaped eyes and Titch glided downward towards them.

On landing back on the bench, she said,

" Well, we got back the two owls."

She then paused, leaving Katie impatiently wait for her to slowly begin again.

" I really do not know how to tell you this. But I think I had better start at the beginning. Albie got it into his head that he needed to find Bobett who was Snizzel's childhood sweetheart because he believed she is the only one who could help him."

"But Mr. Dunken is helping him with his hay fever?" Katie replied in a questioning manner.

"Yes," Titch-Ella said," but the boy is lonely. In spring, summer, and autumn the only places he goes is to the gatherings and the rest of the time he is around here."

Katie took time to think for a moment about Snizzel's feelings and nodded in agreement to what her little friend was telling her. But for now, she was more worried about letting her Mum and Mr. Dunken down by losing Albie and Steamer from the farm.

She could understand why Albie wanted to help his house mate but also Katie was thinking just how selfish Albie was to leave without telling anybody.

"Why did he not let us know where he was going?" She asked the little ones.

Hoaby shrugged his shoulders.

" How am I supposed to know? This is Albie we are talking about; nobody ever knows what he is thinking."

"I think I do," Titch-Ella responded.

"The owls told me he did not want the bats to find out. Especially Vargas, as he would try and stop him; telling him that it would be too dangerous."

"But it is," Katie butted in.

" The owls told me that is why Albie asked them to go with him to protect him from other sky predators, and that is why he asked Steamer to take him on his back. By doing it that way they could fly longer distances at night and he would not be over exposed to the sun for too long. That is why he wanted to put the grease and paint on himself. But the paint would not mix with the grease and because he had so much of it on himself, he kept slipping off Steamers' back. But he had the string tied around the birds' neck to hold on to."

"Wow," Katie said trying to take story all in. She could not decide whether Albie was super clever or super foolish and selfish, but she had no time to judge him, as by listening to the details she knew that Albie's naivety could cook him. She knew that with him covered in grease it would act like a magnifying glass multiplying the effect of the sun and not deterring it. She did not want to upset the little ones with her knowledge, so she asked,

"Where was he when the owls left him?"

"Somewhere near the Donkey Sanctuary over in the direction of a place called Liscarroll, hiding in some foliage with Steamer waiting for the evening to come again so he can continue to fly on towards the town of Charleville, as that is where Bobett is supposed to be."

"Tonight, the bats need to fly," Katie announces," for the owls cannot go back and help as they are putting themselves in real danger by traveling such distances and what would happen if they were caught out in the rain again."

"Yes, I agree" Titch-Ella nodded, "I will go to the attic of the big house and let them know." And with that she flew off leaving Katie and Hoaby with the sleeping owls.

After putting away the feed bags in their proper places, they started collecting the hens' eggs from the many hiding places that the chickens had hatched. It did not take too long as they are not the cleverest when it comes to hiding their eggs as they always lay them in the same places. She put the eggs neatly in an egg tray and they stepped out of the barn making sure the large black doors were firmly clasped.

They then too made their way back towards the house, closing the side gate after they passed though. They felt the mild summer breeze on their face. Katie looked up at the bright sun and the few scattered clouds and thought of Albie asleep in some bush probably tucked up next to the pigeon. She shook her head knowing that there was little they could do except pray that the bats are in time to save him from himself and his thinking. By the time the eggs were put away Titch-Ella had joined them as they checked all the doors to make sure they were well locked this time.

" Snizzel is still asleep," Titch-Ella said as the large front door was pulled closed by Katie. Titch continued talking out her thoughts as they walked away from the big house door towards the bike.

" It is so sad that Snizzel always feels so lonely, even when Mr. Dunken and Albie are here. I just hope that someday we can help Albie to find Bobett or someone like her to help change things for him."

The two little ones jumped into the front carrier basket of the bicycle and Katie started to peddle down the long driveway towards the gate. All three of them looked forward to being back in their nice, homely cottage on top of the hill.

****

14. Carry on Clarance

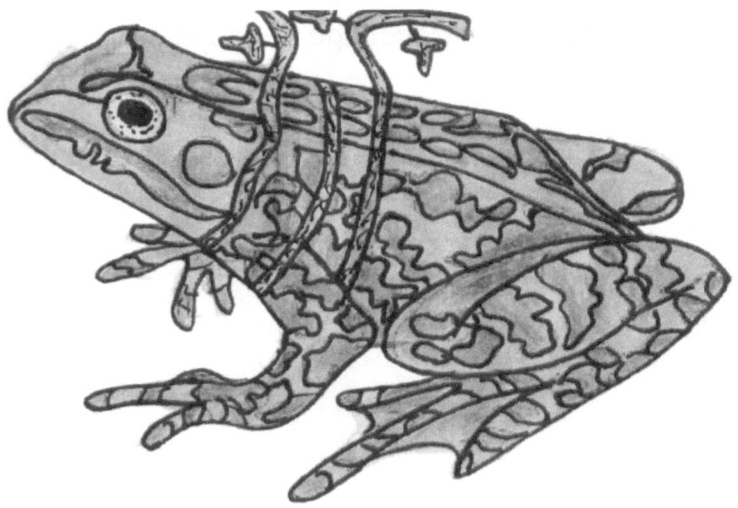

The abnormally high early summer temperatures were hard to bear for most Irish humans with the welcomed swing in May temperatures, just the same as the other extreme bitter cold and snow that the past winter had brought. It was customary for the Irish people to complain about the weather. But, this time, it had even upset the Lepralites, more specifically, Titch-Ella, who found sleeping in the McCarthy's house unbearable even though all the windows were left wide open.

It was well over a month since Albie and his pigeon had disappeared from the farm. She had made it a habit of asking the bats every morning had they found out anything new about them. Every so often, a new bit of information would filter back to her local colony from bats that were based further North of the county as they were obviously tracking the trail of the missing Bobett as he had long passed over the county's boundaries. It was beginning to look like all had become an obsession with him, which she could not understand. Unless he was trying to prove something to the clan or he was genuinely concerned for Snizzel's mental health, but it was all becoming too much for the Lepralites that were following the saga.

After slurping a good amount of water from the gathering barrel, she found her way to her favourite apple tree branch, which she and Hoaby would typically use as a lookout point to view the neighbour's goings-on. However, tonight, it was just a place where she could feel that the house heat was not drying her out. There had been much talk of the thing called global warming. Seemingly, it is a demon created by humans abusing Mother Earth, seemingly now it has returned to eat them all.

Titch-Ella's knowledge of this demon was like everything else learned in the daisy chain effect as she cupped her hands with others in her clan who received it from their Elders after conversing with Mr. Dunken and listening to the human's news. Generally, the Elders would decipher and clean up any information worth passing to the clan members, but they deemed most to be too negative and unnecessary and would bother their clan with it. However, climate change was one bit of news that would impact all nature and humans alike. Lord Dunken had little time for other humans and used words like selfish, greedy, and having no foresight. Maybe he was right. He talked of people spending too much time talking about the demon instead of trying, even in their small ways, to do things that would change this monster's mind about killing us all. He had started damming the stream that passed through his land from the forest behind to the village below to slow the water, trapping it in his fields to create a marsh or wetland that would allow many animals to return to their natural habitat where they lived happily before the land was interfered with, making it arable or workable for farmers. He believed all farmlands should be shared with our wildlife.

But tonight, Titch-Ella just wanted to rest, slumped against the tree's smooth bark. She started to think and ponder her own life. She had an uninterrupted view of the enchanted forever-moving sky and tried to follow the stars as they moved around her world. Many times, unbeknown to anyone else, she asked her earth mother to show her purpose of being so small, living in such a big world, where most of everything is more significant than herself. She questioned how she could make a difference like Mr. Dunken did. How could she make the world a better place? If only she was blessed with a more extensive body or stronger shaped wings, allowing her to fly like a sparrow fast and sharp or even glide like an eagle. Why did she look this way? She knew she was beautiful, but not everyone could at once see that. Like the other day, when Hoaby and her were out exploring the stream, they met a guy called Clarance. At first glance, he giggled at their looks as if he had never met a Lepralite. His first impressions were disappointing for her. However, he looked extraordinary and slimy himself. But after brief introductions and a quick chat, she decided she would like to meet him again. On thinking back, she thought maybe he, too, was beautiful in the eyes of his kind. Her tiredness began dragging her mind toward dreamland. She started thinking of her new family, their love for her and Hoaby, and how their relationship had come a long way, from being caged in the front room to being part of the family. It was a big jump of circumstances in such a short time.

Titch-Ella thought about Ma, her cakes, and her dangerous cat, Digger. She wondered about Geary and hoped he was okay. One day I will teach him how to eat a veggie chicken burger, and he could become a vegetarian. Vegetable burgers could be a game changer in the animal food chain. But that's for another day, she thought as her eyes closed. Her thoughts kept popping up disorganised, coming and going without focus or detail, as like a sand fly was hopping around in her brain, pulling out the memory files. She thought of Donut and how well and quickly his wing had healed, allowing him back flying long distance again. She found herself giggling when she thought of Katie coming home from Dickey Dunken's farm lecturing on her new beliefs that she had learned from the old man. But Adam was patient with her as most Dads are. He did think that Mr. Dunken was a bit OTT at times, whatever that meant.

She kept on smiling as she started to think about Cody. What a clever dog. He knew exactly how to get what he wanted most of the time. Except for the times he stretched Adams's patience to the limit and found himself put outside the back door. Life sure has been strange with the many changes lately. I wonder how Hoaby feels about everything. I know he loves to play with Clive. He is happy with the new living arrangements,

" But I do not know everything. Her mind began to drift again, listening to the night noises. "I want Hoaby to be here with me now. I feel easier when he is around."

Her fractured thoughts were leading her to follow one strange sound.

A strange noise started coming from the forest. Or was it from the stream? Looking out, unable to see very much because of the long grass, Titch-Ella stood up for a closer look, but again, she could only hear the strange noise like burping. Then Hoaby asked.

" Did you hear that? Somebody is calling the rabbits."

"Yes," she said, "that is strange; who would be calling rabbits? Let us go and find out more."

Hoaby was not very enthusiastic after the whole fox escapade up in the forest,

"Do you think it's wise going in there again so soon? He might still be there," he asked.

"Oh, don't be silly, Hoaby. He would be long gone by now," she said, preparing to fly.

She jumped from the tree.

" Come on, slow coach," she teasingly called back at him as she opened her wing flaps to glide towards the forest's edge. The wind was calm but cooling as it passed through her facial fluff. She flew with total freedom, which took her high above everyday life and all her self-doubts. Looking down, she could see the river clearing from the forest. Its water looked appetising. Maybe Hoaby could be right about the fox, she thought as she glided down in wide circles, ensuring no predators were lurking below. She touched down on the stony edge of the river bordering the field. Again, she heard "rabbit" but could not see anything. Then, a long burp,

"What is that?" she stepped away from the high grass in case something might jump out at her. She could feel her feet getting wet as she moved onto the sandy gravel near the water.

Then.

WHAM!

SPLAT!

And spraying dirt, it was her friend who had just landed on his bum after plopping out of the sky and landing in a puddle.

" Hoaby," she squeaked," I'm soaked in mud as she wiped down her kilts. "You are so clumsy,"

"He he he he ho ho ho." she could hear laughter coming closer.

Then.

BOEING!

Out it popped from the river, a big green, grey, slimy wet thing with a vast body that combined a neck and head into one big chunk, with one end being more pointed than the other. That was the head, where its strange eyes sat above the half-moon-shaped smiling-looking mouth. Then she saw what looked like his four chicken legs. At first glance, she thought he was a strange-looking fellow. Hoaby thought he looked just strange, so he decided he did not like him, but it could have been his damaged ego, as it was clear the green thing was laughing at his landing skills or lack thereof.

" Who are you two?" he blurted out, still laughing" You are such strange little creatures?"

Now, he was beginning to upset Titch-Ella as well.

"Who and what are you?" she asked with sharpened tones.

"I am Clarance, your friendly frog," he said, still giggling.

"You are a huge frog. I have not seen such a big frog before," she added.

"Of course, you have not, as I am the only big one in these parts," he declared with pride.

"Where did you come from?" she asked.

"Over there."

He pointed to the other side of the river. Not happy with his flippant answer, she continued, "What do you do?"

"I eat flies," he pushed out his chest more pridefully.

"YUCK!" Hoaby winced, really? "You eat flies?"

"Yes, I do," the frog replied, and in one sudden moment of movement, he spat out his sticky tongue, grabbed a passing fly from the air, and swallowed it," Num Num, that was tasty, Rabbit."

"That's disgusting," Titch-Ella exclaimed with a horrified shiver.

"Well, someone's got to do it," then it gave a long burp of satisfaction.

On settling himself, he asked, "Who are you funny things anyway?

Pushing her hair and wings back, trying to make herself look taller, she said," I am Titch-Ella, and this is Hoaby. We are Lepralites."

"And where are you from?"

Pointing down at the McCarthy house, Hoaby said," Over there" giving back the same limited answers they had received.

Then, thinking momentarily, Titch-Ella asked, "What other tricks can you do?"

"I am very good at hiding. My skin is my camouflage. Nobody can see me anywhere! I bet you could not see me as you flew down here?"

"No, we did not see you," Titch-Ella agreed.

Seeing how well he thought of himself and with Titch-Ella still intrigued by the strange, oversized frogs' activities, she asked, "What else can you do?"

He blew out his chest again, filling it with wind and pride.

"I am by far the best jumper on the river, for nobody can match me! Watch me!"

And with a long burp, he bounced into the air, hopping from rock to rock.

BOEING.

BOEING.

He was over to the other side and back in little time.

" Rabbit Rabbit, what did you think of that?"

Hoaby stepped in with his question.

"Why are you always calling out to the Rabbits?"

"No, I don't," Clarance replied, "I say Ribbit."

"Ok, what's a ribbit so?"

"I don't know. That's just what I say. I have always said ribbit. All frogs say ribbit."

He, too, now was getting a bit annoyed by their question-laden conversation.

Realising that the frog was heading for a bad mood, Titch-Ella said, "Yes, you are a perfect jumper. Are you good at all games?" she asked, "for I have an amazing game that I think you would be good at?"

She knew that his self-righteousness would not let her down, for he was far too full of pride to back out of any game that she might plan, and he did not disappoint,

"Of course, I'm good at all games! What game do you have in mind?"

Hoaby knew she was again weaving her words to get what she wanted.

"Showjumping," she declared." It is a game that the humans play. They put up stick fences, get up on their horse, and ride them around in circles, hopping over the fences."

"That's a silly game," Hoaby said, butting into her plans, "We have no horses or sticks."

"No, but we have Clarance."

She was now beginning to show a bit of her pride of her own. Clarance looked confused, but he agreed, still unsure of what game he was about to play. Hoaby was bewildered by his lack of understanding of his friend's thoughts and was very cautious, as her games had a history of bruising him. But before a debate started, she said, "Hoaby, you go get some bindweed to use as a bridal for the horse, I mean the frog."

"What is bindweed?" he asked,

"It's the long stringy ivy-like plant with the pink flower over there in the hedging." Pointing toward a ditch not too far away, again, her little blue-haired foot soldier obliged, and it was not long before Titch-Ella was stripping the string of its flowers and leaves.

"Now Clarance, you stand still when I wrap your bridal around your neck."

After a brief look, trying to decide where his neck was, she said, "Around your body, I mean."

Clarance was still confused by her antics but stood still as he wrapped up like a parcel. She wrapped it around and around until it was all used. Then she tied it.

"Now. That looks good," she thought, standing back, putting her hands on her hips like Mum did, admiring her work. Clarance tried to puff out his chest but could not, as it was too tightly wrapped, and he could only offer a light, "Ribbit, what now?"

"You keep still. I will climb up on your back, and we will practice by hopping from stone to stone and gliding over the water jumps. So let us begin."

Up she hopped.

She got hold of the bindweed bridal while sitting on his back. Hoaby looked at her, wondering what was coming next.

" Ok. Are you ready, Clarance?" she asked as she kicked his belly.

BOEING!

Straight up!

Then sideways!

Up and down!

He jumped until she was tossed into the stream.

Hoaby started laughing but then saw her staring at him angrily, so he abruptly stopped, keeping his laughter on the inside of his mouth, thinking, how miss precious Princess looked with her scraggy wet hair and a saggy kilt!

Again, she was standing with her hands on her hips, but it was far from the pride she felt as she glared at Hoaby.

Clarance was happy, jinking and shouting excitedly, "I love this showjumping game; it's fantastic!

"THAT was not show jumping," Titch-Ella declared angrily." That was bronco bull riding."

She was fuming with annoyance.

"That makes sense," said Clarance, "for I am not a horse frog. I am a bullfrog, ribbit."

"Ok," she replied as her frustrations grew. "Why did you not tell me that before?"

Titch-Ella was not going to let this game get the better of her.

"Ok, then, we will play bull riding."

"What's that?" Hoaby asked, still smirking,

"That is where YOU get up on the bull that is Clarance, and he starts hopping and jumping around the way we just did, and I will count one, two, three, and so on until he throws you off."

His smirk turned to concern as she continued to explain her game.

"It is your job to hold on as long as possible until I count to thirty. Then you win, and his job is to get rid of you before I reach thirty. It's easy. I just did it."

Then she paused to consider amplifying her accomplishments and finished by saying, "Except you didn't count! So, we will never know just how good I was?!"

Hoaby could see she was building attitude but knew he would be wasting his time arguing with her, as she was always one step ahead of him with her words. Whether she was right or wrong, and even if he did get to win one of these arguments, she would stop him and ask,

" Do you want to be correct, or do you want to be happy?"

The few times he did persist with those arguments, Titch-Ella would stop talking to him, and he did not like that at all, as it made him feel lonely. He didn't want to disappoint her, even though he expected the worst, so he climbed up on the bullfrog's back.

"What do I do now?" he asked.

"You hold on tight," she said, walking around the back of them.

"Are you ready?" she asked.

As he nodded, she slapped Clarance's bum.

BOOM!

Up he went.

Down, sideways, bouncing and hopping for all he was worth.

Like an uncoiled spring, he sprung, holding on with all his strength. Hoaby could hear Titch-Ella shout," …twelve, thirteen…."

Then he flew.

Still holding the weed in his hand, he and the bullfrog parted company. He descended headfirst into the deep patch of slurred mud on the riverbank. At first, Titch-Ella was very concerned for his safety until she saw his upstanding flat feet begin to wiggle. Then she started thinking about just how dangerous the game was; she found herself saying,

" That's not good."

Clarance was elated with joy, hopping, and jumping around the riverbank.

"I won. I won. Ribbit Ribbit. Can we do it again, can we?"

An overwhelming guilt caught hold of Titch-Ellas's thoughts about how she had treated her best friend. She ran to help him as he struggled to get back up and cleaned the mud from his cheeky, furry face.

" Maybe another time. I think we all need a wash." And she ended the game.

She began to hear the wind making a sniffing noise. She looked around but could not see anything. Then something nibbled on her ear. Reflexing, she pushed it away and turned into two kitten squirrels kissing her face. She must have fallen asleep. As she woke up, Titch-Ella began to think how sad it was that she was just too big to ride a bullfrog. "It is a pity that I am not two inches smaller?"

As she felt the love of the little kit squirrels playing around her, she asked herself, "are we all born the wrong size, or do we all look so strange? I do not think so. But, for now, I can start improving the world by telling my family, how great they are and how I appreciate them be in my life."

She hugged the two little squirrels, jumped down from the tree, and called out, "Hoaby."

****

A Time for Lepralites

About the Authors

AngJon Hornibrook are a husband-and-wife team, living near the Atlantic Ocean in County Cork, Ireland.

Joined by Deirdre Tobin, Angele and Jonathan bring the magic of their imaginations together.

Angele is originally from Lithuania and worked as a care assistant until she required a break for health reasons. She has now found much joy in illustrating and bringing the Lepralites and other characters to life using her traditional pen and paper sketches interpreting the writings of her husband Jonathan and her friend Deirdre.

Jonathan is originally from County Cork and has worked in the Construction Industry for many years, but now enjoys his time developing and drafting stories using his strange in depth, often humorous and tilted views of his creations.

Deirdre is originally from Co. Waterford, Ireland but has lived in Cork for 30 years. She works in the Pharmaceutical Industry. Using her natural attention to detail she organises the creativity into manuscript, adding in her own skills to the project to develop the finished product you see today. Combining this with her marketing skills allows the AngJon stories to be brought to everyone's attention.

We, at AngJon, hope you found joy in our creations and storylines.

To find out more, Join us at

www.lepralites.com

****

www.ingramcontent.com/pod-product-compliance
Lightning Source LLC
Chambersburg PA
CBHW020107180626
46812CB00006B/2502